MW00512326

Skip
Coryell

Stalking Natalie

Never ride the elevator alone …

Published by White Feather Press, LLC in 2009

ISBN   978-0-9822487-5-1

Printed in the United States of America

Back cover photo ©iStockphoto.com/Brett Gage
Front cover photo ©iStockphoto.com/Nathan Maxfield
Interior cover photo ©iStockphoto.com/Denis Raev

White Feather Press

Reaffirming Faith in God, Family, and Country!

Prologue

Natalie Katrell was a single mother. Her daughter, six-year old Amethyst, seemed like a miniature copy of herself, with long, blonde hair, shining blue eyes, and a smile that softened the hearts of most people who looked upon her. But neither Natalie nor Amethyst could see the man watching them. He always stayed off in the shadows, hidden around corners, or gazing from behind the innocent pages of a paperback book. Sometimes he sipped tea while at other times he nursed a vanilla latte with a double shot of espresso. But always, without fail, he watched Natalie and her daughter. He was obsessed and Natalie was his next chosen one.

Chapter One

Natalie flinched as she pulled the trigger, sending the shot downrange safely into the sand berm but nowhere near the target. Her back was arched to the rear and her arms locked tightly out in front of her as she tried to get as far away from the gun as possible. Sam Colton nodded knowingly. He'd seen this many times before, always with new shooters. He let his student finish firing out the cylinder before lying to her.

"Not bad, Natalie, not bad for a first time."

Natalie looked over at the older man in disbelief and slumped her shoulders in discouragement.

"But I didn't even hit the paper!"

Sam chuckled out loud.

"Yes, but you didn't shoot me either. I'd say that's a pretty good start."

He reached out in front of her and carefully removed the Smith and Wesson 38 caliber revolver from her hand. He casually opened the cylinder, tipped it back, and pressed the ejector rod once, letting the empty brass casings fall to the grass.

Natalie folded her arms across her chest, indicating a closed posture. Sam made note of it as he reloaded her revolver.

"At this point I don't expect you to hit the paper. I just want you to get acquainted with your gun, kind of like you would a new puppy."

Natalie squinted her eyes at the old man suspiciously.

"A new puppy?'

Sam nodded.

"Yup. That's what I said."

He handed the pistol back to her.

"Now let's try it again. But this time, instead of aiming, I want you to point the gun at the berm and just squeeze off the shots as quickly as you can."

Natalie looked at him with one raised eyebrow.

"You serious?"

Sam nodded.

"Yup."

"Well what if I don't hit anything?"

Sam smiled.

"Doesn't matter. Besides, there's no such thing as not hitting anything. The bullet always goes somewhere and always hits something. Just keep the muzzle pointed downrange and don't let it hit *me*."

Natalie nodded her head, waited a few seconds as if regaining her composure, and then raised the revolver up and fired one round. She closed her eyes and flinched.

"Don't stop! Keep shooting!"

She hesitated and fired again. Sam yelled at her.

"Faster! Shoot faster!"

Natalie's gun barked out again and again until it finally clicked on an empty chamber. She slowly lowered the gun.

"Did I hit anything?"

Sam nodded.

"Yup. Sure did. There's lots of dead air and dirt downrange."

Natalie handed him the empty gun and Sam began to empty the brass and quickly reload.

"You want to tell me why I'm doing this? It seems like a waste of expensive ammunition."

"Yup. Sure would seem that way wouldn't it. But it ain't."

He handed the loaded firearm back to her and pointed downrange.

"This time I want you to close your eyes and just feel the recoil. Get used to it. Make friends with the power."

The ends of Natalie's long, blonde hair waved in the breeze but the rest was held in place by her shooting muffs and safety glasses. She was about 3 inches taller than Sam, not to mention slender, shapely and attractive. She reminded Sam of his oldest daughter, Karen, who lived in Oregon.

"But isn't shooting with your eyes closed dangerous?"

"Depends on where the muzzle's pointed. You just keep the bullets headed down range, don't turn around, and everything will be just fine. I'm watching you. Trust me."

Natalie tentatively raised her gun and pointed it down range. She closed her eyes, then peeked through one eyelid.

"Stop cheating, Natalie. I may be old, but I'm not blind. Leastwise not yet."

Natalie hesitated and then closed her eyes. She gripped the gun so hard her knuckles turned white.

"Just relax now girl. Relax and press steady and slow to the rear."

Bang!

The gun went off and Natalie quickly opened her eyes again. But Sam quickly rebuked her.

"Close yer eyes!"

"But I want to see where the bullet went."

"It don't matter where the bullet went so long as I'm not bleeding! Now shoot again."

Bang!

"Again. Shoot again!"

Bang! Bang!

"Good. Now one more time."

Bang!

Natalie lowered the gun and opened her eyes. She looked downrange and checked the target for holes. She let out a disappointed sigh when she saw the unblemished paper.

"I missed again."

Sam laughed out loud.

"So what did you expect? You had your eyes closed."

Natalie handed him the gun.

"Oh, I don't know. I thought maybe it was some kind of Zen trick or something. You know, *Use the force, Luke!*"

Sam reloaded the gun before handing it back to her.

"The only thing that works is focus and practice. Now point the gun downrange and empty it. Feel the recoil. Shake hands with the power."

Natalie nodded and did as she was told. When the gun was empty she handed it back to her instructor and he reloaded it.

"How long are we going to do this?"

Sam handed her back the loaded pistol.

"Until you're not afraid of the gun anymore."

Natalie scoffed out loud.

"This gun could kill me! I'm supposed to be afraid of it!"

Sam shook his head in disagreement.

"Wrong thinking! Wrong talking, girl! Never fear the gun unless it's pointed at you. Respect the gun. Never fear it!"

Natalie nodded her head in slight understanding. She fired the gun until it was empty before handing it back to him. For the next 20 minutes, Sam reloaded and Natalie closed her eyes and fired downrange. Eventually, her grip loosened slightly and the recoil bothered her less.

"Now, on this next round of fire, I want you to open your eyes and aim the best you can at the center of the bulls eye."

"What if I miss?"

"Then I won't have to change the target and it costs me less money. Either way, one of us wins."

Natalie smiled softly for the first time that night. She turned back to the target, raised her arms and took aim.

Bang!

This time she didn't flinch, and there was a bullet hole on the outside edge of the paper.

"Hey! I hit it!"

Sam nodded.

"Yup. Now lean into your shot a little more. Get closer to the gun."

Natalie leaned in closer, took careful aim, and fired off another round. The next bullet was 2 inches closer to the bulls eye. A huge smile spread across her face.

"I'm closer now."

Sam nodded.

"Yup. Try it again."

Natalie raised her arms up.

"Bend your knees a bit. Don't stiffen up. Relax."

Bang!

The bullet hole was just outside the center ring.

"Hey! Did you see that?"

Sam pointed downrange.

"Don't get cocky. Try it again."

Bang!

"Hey! Look at that! I hit the bulls eye!"

Sam reached over and firmly removed the pistol from Natalie's hand.

"I've got it."

"But I still have one bullet left!"

Sam shook his head back and forth. He opened the cylinder and unloaded the gun. He put the single, live round back into his pocket, while allowing the empty brass to fall to the ground.

"It don't matter. Your time is up."

Natalie looked over at him in disbelief. She put her hands on her hips when she spoke.

"You mean to tell me that we don't have time for one more shot?"

Sam nodded.

"Yup. That's what I mean. Now go down there and get yer target and meet me back at the benchrest."

Natalie stood her ground, but Sam turned and walked away. She watched him a moment, but then moved down to the target and admired her bulls eye. She carefully took down the paper and rolled it up before heading back to the benchrest with Sam.

"Now I want you to practice your dry firing every day. Make sure the gun is unloaded. Double check it to be sure. Don't even be in the same room with live ammo. Understand?"

"Yes, Sam. I'm not stupid."

Sam barked right back.

"No one is stupid until they shoot themselves. Just be careful, girl."

Natalie's smile was barely discernible. She was starting to get used to the old man's bark.

"I'll be careful old man."

Sam grunted out loud and turned to walk away.

"See you next Tuesday. And who you calling old man? I'm still in my prime!"

Sam's grumblings faded away as Natalie carefully placed her revolver in its case. As she turned and walked off the range, she felt proud of that lone bulls eye.

But, off in the distance she didn't see the other man put away his binoculars. He had a concerned look on his face, as if he didn't like what he was seeing. He got into his car and drove away, thinking about what to do about it.

Chapter Two

-May 21st-

I woke up again this morning with that taste in my mouth and that smell on my clothes. I have no idea where it's coming from and that bothers me. That just doesn't seem normal. Maybe I should ask somebody about that? But who would I ask? There is no one but him, and he disgusts me! He would probably just lie to me anyway. But still . . . he is my brother . . . my only friend. Is that normal, to have only one friend I mean?

I see other people, everyone I suppose, who walk around laughing, talking to one another, pretending to like each other and I wonder if they're really having fun, or is it all just an act like I do? Are some people really happy? And, if so, how do they do that? It confuses me. Sometimes I think that I'd like to be that way too, assuming that it's real and not something phony. But how do I know for sure? Sometimes I wonder why I'm even here? Why is anyone here?

Mark set his pen down on his desk and looked up at the disgusting orange cubicle wall in front of him. He looked over at Natalie across the aisle and tried not to stare too hard. She was beautiful, and he wanted to talk to her, but he could never manage more than a few words at a time. Natalie was one of the pretty people. He knew that. He could tell just by the way she carried herself, by the way she talked, formed her words, by the way she smiled, and, especially, by the way her eyes paid attention to the person she was talking to. She had done it once with him as well, in the elevator, just the two of them. It had been after hours during a business crunch time. Natalie had been asked to stay late, but Mark had not. He stayed anyway, just to be close to her, just to watch the way she wrapped her long, blonde hair around her right forefinger and twirled it while she was thinking.

Mark liked everything about Natalie. She glanced up from her computer screen, but he quickly looked back down at his notebook. She looked at him for just a second before returning her gaze to the monitor in front of her. Mark began to write again.

> *She just looked at me again. I wonder what that means? Does she like me? Maybe she just saw me staring at her? I hope not. I've noticed that people get nervous when I stare at them. I don't mean any harm. I just like looking at people, studying them, watching them talk and interact. Maybe it will give me a clue as to how I can become more like them. That would be nice. Well, I have to get back to work now, but I'll write more later on my next break. I get to format and proofread fifty pages of a technical manual on the hydraulic lift unit on a garbage truck. It's really quite fascinating. I love my job! Good bye for now.*

> *Signed - Striving to be normal.*

Mark closed the green, spiral notebook, opened the drawer to the right of his chair and placed it inside. He quietly closed and locked the drawer, then returned the key to its place on the chain around his neck. His eyes went back down to the white-paper printout of the technical manual in front of him and he began to read.

"Using a crane or forklift to support the hydraulic cylinder, remove the pin locking bolts to free the cylinder. "

Mark smiled as he moved his hand down from his forehead and scribbled a neat proofreader's mark, transposing the words "pin" and "locking" to correct the error. It made him feel good to find something wrong and make it right. The very act of it gave his life purpose and meaning. He continued to read, finding more errors, marking them up, and then reading some more.

Natalie watched Mark from across the aisle, amazed that anyone could actually enjoy this job. She did it only to pay the rent, and to buy food for herself and her daughter, Amethyst. It was the most boring and pointless job she'd ever had, but she had been here, dead-ended ever since her daughter's birth and her boyfriend's abandonment. She could still hear her mother's warnings echoing back from the past: "Don't give away the milk for free or he'll never buy the cow. Why should he? All men are alike. They'll just use you and then move on."

Natalie hated it when her mother was right. In her heart, she knew that all men couldn't be that way. Just because Jim had abandoned her shortly after her daughter's birth, that meant nothing in and of itself. It was just a fluke. In reality, there were lots of exciting, loyal, attractive and sexy men out there who would love to share life with her and Amethyst. Problem was ...

She looked across the aisle again at Mark. He was attractive enough, but, weird as can be. Maybe he was an alien? How could a human enjoy these working conditions? It just wasn't right. It wasn't natural. Natalie pursed her lips together in disgust. There he is again, smiling. She watched as Mark reached down and scribbled another proofreader's mark. He's so chivalrous. Look at him, he's slain another dangling participle.

Natalie quietly buried her face in her palms for a moment, then she girded up her courage, picked up her pen, and began proofing the accuracy of an electric schematic to the Semper Deluxe can opener, model 367a125.

It was 2:30PM. Just 2 more hours and she could pick up Amethyst and start living her real life. This job wasn't real; it was just a dream, a nightmare that she lived out everyday to support her daughter. Why hadn't she majored in business like her mother had told her? But no! She never listened to Mom. Never! Because her mother was boring and practical, and she had this whiny voice that just grated on her nerves like one of those high-pitched dentist drills.

The digital clock on her desk dropped down another number. 2:31PM. Just one hour and 59 minutes and she could leave.

Mark stared at her from across the aisle. She was so beautiful. He just couldn't stop. Natalie felt his eyes and glanced up without warning. She saw Mark looking at her and frowned.

"Will you please stop staring at me!"

The moment the words left her mouth, she regretted saying them, but it was too late. Natalie watched as hurt filled his eyes and then he tore his face back down to the white paper in front of him. He looked like a wounded puppy. The damage was done.

Natalie got up from her chair and walked the thirty feet to the restroom. She closed and locked the door behind her. For a few minutes she cried, then washed her face with cold water and returned to her desk. She hated this job and quietly scolded herself for not majoring in business.

Mark saw her return to her desk out of the corner of his eye, but forced himself to keep reading. Instead, he kept his head down and searched diligently for more errors, fulfilling his purpose, finding things wrong and making them right. From now on, he would be more discreet.

Chapter Three

"The latest in a string of four rape-murders occurred last night on the east side of town once again rendering the city terrified and afraid to go out at night."

Natalie reclined on the couch in her living room apartment nursing a small bowl of vanilla ice cream and listening to the news. An involuntary chill ran up her spine when she heard of the latest murder. She placed the ice cream on the coffee table to her left and pulled the blanket up tighter against her chest. The serial killings were what had prompted her to buy a pistol and start classes with Sam Colton just last week.

"Chief of Police Gary Frank refused to elaborate on earlier comments, only reiterating that the full resources of the department were on the case and that he would not rest until the killer was brought to justice. When asked if the FBI was actively involved in the case, he declined comment."

Natalie nodded her head in agreement. She hadn't been sleeping much either, and perhaps that's why she'd been so short with her coworker today. Mark was annoying to her, but he hadn't deserved her rebuke. Tomorrow she would apologize. She glanced over at the apartment door to make sure the dead bolt and chain was securely in place. Sam Colton had given her a long list of things to help protect and deter from an attack.

Her doors were triple-locked, even the glass slider. Her pistol was loaded and readily accessible inside the gun safe. She'd also put a large dog dish and chewed-up bone on the balcony in front of the slider. She would have gotten a real dog, but they were a nuisance to her, always needing to be walked and pooped and fed. Her life was already complicated and busy enough with just her and Amethyst.

"And now we welcome our guest, Tom Evans, former FBI profiler and author of *Serial Killings of the Twentieth Century*. Good evening Tom. Thanks for joining us."

The man was old, with silver hair and wire-rimmed spectacles. He nodded formally.

"Thank you, Jane. It's my pleasure."

The TV anchor, Jane Reynolds, was a beautiful, thin, sophisticated woman in her early thirties, wearing a red skirt and a black and red plaid top. Natalie shook her head from side to side as she spoke.

"That outfit looks atrocious! There's no way I would wear that on television!"

Natalie reached over to her left and picked up her ice cream again. Amethyst was already in bed, so she had broken out a pint of the expensive ice cream, the kind with real vanilla flavoring.

"So tell us, Mr. Evans, do you believe this is the work of a bona fide serial killer?"

The elder man in the brown tweed jacket nodded his head immediately.

"Without a doubt, Jane. He fits the profile to the letter, and I have no doubt that he will continue to rape and murder until he is caught or until he is killed."

Jane Reynolds hesitated a moment before responding.

"Until he is killed? What do you mean by that? Who would kill him? Would he commit suicide or are you talking about vigilantes? Please elaborate for our viewers."

"I mean exactly that, Jane. I doubt this man will stop until he's dead or incapacitated in some way. He is a determined and dedicated killer of high intelligence and pays meticulous attention to detail, sometimes surveilling his victims for months before striking. I wouldn't be surprised to know that he's already chosen his next victim."

Jane nodded her head and pressed him for more details.

"So what about suicide? Do many serial killers resort to that?"

Tom shrugged his shoulders.

"Sure, some do, names like Karl Denke, Herbert Baumeister, and John Wayne Glover come to mind, but not as many as we'd like obviously. Indeed, history has shown that some serial killers do resort to suicide, but typically not until they sense the police are closing in and their reign of terror is about to end or after they have already been imprisoned. In that regard, they're a lot like people who go on a shooting rampage."

"So is there anything special about this particular case that fascinates you, Mr. Evans?"

The man thought for a moment, and crossed his right leg over his left knee before answering.

'I think if I had to guess, I'd say that this man, despite his dedication and the brutally violent nature of his crimes ... I'd say this man still feels some conflict, perhaps even some remorse at what he's doing. It's almost as if a part of him enjoys the killing, is compelled by it and can't stop, while another part of him, is ashamed and wants to make amends afterwards."

"Ashamed? How so?"

The serial killer expert was on his soapbox now and seemed to be enjoying his moment in the sun.

"It's the way he tidies up the crime scene and the bodies

afterwards. An inside source has even told me that he left a note of apology at two of the four murder scenes. At any rate, even if this man wants to stop killing, he won't be able to. The killing is a drug to him and he is hopelessly addicted to the feeling. Many drug addicts and alcoholics want to quit, and feel remorse and shame afterwards, but unless they get proper, professional help, they never do. They can't. The sickness runs too deep. It's a part of them."

Natalie found herself shivering on the couch, and she quickly changed the channel to the Food Network where they were making chocolate-covered strawberries.

Leaving the television playing, Natalie got up from the couch and walked over to her daughter's bedroom door. She opened the door a crack and peeked inside to make sure she was okay. She watched closely to make sure that Amethyst's chest was rising and falling with each breath. She did that every night just to make sure her daughter was okay. It reassured her, and she didn't sleep well herself unless she knew for sure that her daughter was breathing well.

There was always this impending sense of doom in Natalie's mind, as if she were the mother of all Chicken Littles. First, her father had died when she was 12, then her sister just 2 years after that. Then, during college she had met Jim, the love of her life, or so she'd thought. He had pledged his life to her, but because of issues from his childhood, he'd wanted to wait on marriage. They'd moved in together and then Amethyst was born. Natalie had been ecstatic, but Jim had changed after that. A few months later he left with no explanation or warning. That was almost 6 years ago and she hadn't heard from him since. With the help of her mother, she'd managed to finish college and get her BA in English, but her dreams of being a writer were dashed. There was no more time for her dream. She was a single parent now.

In the end, she'd taken the job at Amanatech out of financial necessity, and now she was just waiting for the next shoe to drop, for the next crisis to befall her life. It was a terrible way to live, but she couldn't seem to stop thinking that way. She recalled several years back, when she was having trouble coping with Jim's abandonment and the realities of being a single parent, Natalie had gone to see a counselor. She remembered the session like it was only yesterday.

"So why, Natalie, why do you feel like something terrible is going to happen to your baby?"

Natalie looked up at her therapist as if that was the most patently absurd question he could ask. When she answered, there was a bitter edge to her voice.

"Hmm, let me see, maybe it's because that's what has always happened to me before? Maybe it's because my sister died of cancer, my father was beaten to death in a truckstop restroom, and the only man I ever loved and the father of my child left me without explanation or warning? What do you think? Do you think that might have something to do with it?"

The middle-aged therapist shifted in his chair but his eyes never left her own. Natalie hated it when he stared at her like that.

"So are you going to go through the rest of your life like Chicken Little, believing that the sky could fall on you at any moment? Is that realistic, Natalie? Is that the way you want to live?" He paused for a moment, waiting for her response but none came so he continued. "And what about this ceiling, Natalie? Is the ceiling here in this room going to fall on you?"

Natalie smiled.

"If it does, you can bet I'll never come in here again."

The therapist returned a slight smile.

"Okay, I'll give you that much. We have to learn from our experiences, but we have to hold on to reason as well."

Natalie looked down at her folded hands on her lap.

"So are you calling me irrational?"

"What do you think, Natalie? Do you think you're being irrational?"

Natalie's face flushed red and she lashed out with her typical lack of restraint.

"Will you just cut the psycho crap and answer my question! Do you think I'm irrational?"

At first, the man was taken aback by her outburst, but he quickly masked his surprise and regained his composure.

"We'll come back to that in a moment. But let's say, just for the sake of illustration, that this ceiling does fall in on us. But then I repair the ceiling, and this time I reinforce it with steel girders and the strongest concrete known to man. The ceiling is two feet thick and impervious to earthquake and even tornados. What would you say then, Natalie?"

Natalie looked up from her lap and responded without a moment's hesitation.

"The next time it caves in it'll kill me!"

And that's how Natalie had learned of her paranoia. True, she'd lived a hard life and it was merited, to some degree. But Natalie had admitted to herself that she walked around everyday expecting to be mugged, to be struck by a car, to be attacked by radical Islamic terrorists. In short, sooner or later, the sky above her was bound to fall. Why not? It always had before?

But the therapist had been wrong. She wasn't irrational ... just cautious, like a frog in a blender, and she never knew when

God was going to hit the power switch.

And that's why Natalie watched her daughter so carefully, because she wanted to protect her from the same disastrous misfortunes that had invaded her own life. That's why she was learning to shoot a gun; why she looked outside before stepping through doors, why she never talked to strangers, and why she seldom made friends. Natalie was isolated, because that was the only way to protect herself. She couldn't protect herself from God, but she could defend against other people. Natalie was alienated. She was lonely, and yes, she was even irrational. But it was all her own choice. The walls were of her own making.

She looked down at her little daughter and smiled softly. Then she walked quietly to her bedside and knelt down. Slowly, barely touching her, she stroked her daughter's beautiful, blonde hair. Amethyst's eyes flickered and then opened slowly.

"I'm tired Mommy."

Natalie bent down and hugged her.

"I'm sorry honey. I was just checking on you."

Amethyst reached her left hand out from beneath the covers and stroked her mother's face.

"Don't worry Mommy. I'll be okay."

Natalie smiled and gave her a kiss on the forehead.

"Thanks honey. Now get back to sleep. I love you."

"I love you too, Mommy."

And then Natalie stood up and reluctantly backed away and out the door, watching her daughter's face receding into the shadows as she went. She closed the door, all the while, hoping above hope, praying to God, that the ceiling would not give way during the night.

Chapter Four

-May 22nd-

I drove in to work early this morning, and I heard that Michael W. Smith song on the radio again. The words always make me cry, so I'm glad I don't hear it very often. It goes something like this:

"Looking for a reason, roaming through the night to find, my place in this world, my place in this world. Not a lot to lean on, I need your light to help me find, my place in this world, my place in this world."

Sometimes I feel like I have no place in this world, like I don't belong here, like I'm the designated freak, put here only so others can feel more normal.

I don't like it, and it makes me wonder why ...

And sometimes I think about God and I wonder ...

Why am I here? Why would God even make me?
Do I exist solely to make wrong things right?

Can there be any reason for the existence of a person without friends? If a person falls in the forest, and no one is there to hear him cry, is he really there? Does he even exist?

Mark lowered his pen once more and stared blankly at the orange fabric wall in front of him. It was the most sickening orange he'd ever seen. He was so absorbed in his own self-pity that he hadn't seen Natalie stop beside his desk.

"Mark?"

He continued to stare blankly.

"Mark? Can I talk to you a moment?"

He jumped in his chair when he saw her and quickly grabbed his notebook and closed it. He didn't say anything in reply.

"Mark, do you have a moment?"

Mark stared straight ahead, not moving. Natalie thought that was odd, but she forged on regardless.

"I just wanted to apologize to you for my impatience yesterday. I didn't mean anything by it."

Mark said nothing.

"It's just that I've been under a lot of stress lately and I guess it's getting the best of me."

No response from Mark.

"Anyway, I just wanted to say I'm sorry and that it won't happen again."

For several more seconds, Natalie stood there, waiting for a response. Finally, Mark swiveled slowly to his left, with his head still lowered. He nodded slightly.

"So, do you forgive me?"

Marked waited a moment and then nodded slowly once up and down. Natalie was starting to feel clumsy, so she set the envelope on his desk.

"This is for you. My daughter drew the picture. I hope you like it."

And then Natalie turned and walked back to her desk, got her coffee cup and headed awkwardly away to the break room on the far side of the building. Halfway down the aisle she looked over her shoulder and saw Mark still staring down with a blank look on his face. She shook her head from side to side. He was the weirdest guy she'd ever seen.

After Natalie was out of sight, Mark turned back to his desk, opened his notebook and began writing again.

But if someone were to acknowledge me, if another person were to recognize that I exist, then, would I be any more real? Would I be valid? If I fell in the forest, and a friend was with me, then she would hear me fall, and I would become real.

Mark glanced over at the envelope. It was light blue with embossed flowers on it. It looked expensive. Slowly, he placed his pen down on the desk and carefully moved his hand over to the paper envelope. He touched it. It was real.

The words of the song whispered through his head again.

"*Looking for a reason, roaming through the night to find, my place in this world, my place in this world.*"

Did he have a place in this world? Was there a reason to live? Was there anyone to be his friend?

Slowly, and carefully, as if the paper would crumble with too much pressure, he slid his left forefinger under the envelope, placed his thumb on top, and lifted it to his face. He looked down the aisle both ways and saw no one coming. He raised the envelope to his nose and smelled the paper. There was the slightest scent of Natalie on it. A smile almost touched his lips.

Mark opened his pencil drawer and brought out a letter opener. He slid the blade under the fold and the paper cut easily. Slowly, almost in fear, he looked inside and then pulled out the card stock paper. It was plain white, and there was a picture of two stick figures on it. One had long hair and the other had short hair. One wore a dress and the other pants. In neat, cursive writing, were the words " I'm sorry, Mark. Have a good day!"

He heard someone coming down the aisle, so he quickly shoved the card back inside the envelope and placed it beneath the notebook in front of him.

Natalie paused for a moment before setting her coffee down. She glanced over at Mark, but he was turned away from her. She sat down, took one sip of her coffee and then began to check her email.

Across the aisle, Mark looked at her from the corner of his eye, but only for a second. He locked his notebook inside his drawer and turned on his monitor, all the while, feeling just a tiny bit more real than yesterday.

Chapter Five

"It's not natural to want to take the life of another human, but some people do it. Some even enjoy it. I personally believe that most people, given the right situation, are capable of taking another human life."

Natalie sat in her chair along with the other fifteen students in the personal protection class. About half the students were women and the other half men. When Natalie heard Sam Colton's last comment, she involuntarily shook her head slightly from side to side. Then she caught herself and stopped abruptly before looking around to make sure no one had noticed. The lady next to her was still shaking her head back and forth.

Sam Colton smiled knowingly and thought to himself. *It's almost always the women. They just don't have the stomach for it.* He took a deep breath and forged ahead with the tough-sell idea of killing a man from close up.

"Yes, I know what you're thinking. I've seen it before, many times in fact, but I'm here to tell you that all of you have an animal side. Every last one of you, the women included, have what it takes to pull the trigger and kill a man."

Sam gazed around the room, assessing his audience, choosing his words carefully, being careful not to push them too far too soon.

"You've all heard me say that a firearm is a tool of last resort, but some day, somewhere, someone is going to stick a gun in your face and demand something that you're not willing to give, whether it be your life, the life of your son or daughter, or your husband or wife, or maybe they just want to rape you and leave you dead on the roadside."

Sam paced slowly back and forth, choosing his words carefully, watching their response and pushing it as far as he dared.

"All of you have to decide when you will take a life and when you will not. It's too late when the knife is already in your face, because you won't be able to think rationally and you just won't have the time."

Natalie stopped taking notes for a moment and just listened. She was starting to like the old man. He was interesting, and being taught by him was kind of like sitting on a porch swing with the grandfather she never knew.

"Let's take a few minutes to talk about what happens to your body during a life-and-death conflict. The first thing that happens is your heart rate skyrockets. This is due to a huge amount of adrenaline that your body dumps into your bloodstream in anticipation of a fight. My "at rest" heart rate is about 60 beats per minute. That's fairly slow. But things quickly change when stress is added. When the adrenaline surge happens, I can feel it immediately, and it's almost impossible to control it once it's started.

"When your pulse gets up to about 90, that's when your brain is functioning at its best. You are on high-alert status, and there is extra oxygen being pumped to your brain and the rest of your body. But once the heart rate gets above 110, nasty things start to happen.

"As soon as your brain realizes that you are in danger, it constricts the blood vessels leading to your extremities. This is done, so that if you are cut, for example on your arm, then it will take longer for you to bleed to death, and you can defend your-self for a longer period of time. Because of the lack of blood in your hands, your wrists may tingle and your fingers may feel a certain amount of numbness and freezing cold. Suddenly, very simple things, like ejecting a magazine, or even pulling back a pistol slide, can become very difficult to do.

"Your brain is also affected; it reverts to a primitive state of mind, where complex thinking and reasoning is next to impos-sible. At this point, most people can think but one thing: "Oh my god! That's a gun! I'm going to die!

"Yet, despite all these physiological realities coming into play, it is still possible for you to survive a gun fight. If you can control them, harness them, then all these things will work for you. However, if you allow the adrenaline, increased pulse, and oxygen supply to run rampant with no thought to self control, then you will be reduced to a throbbing mass of blood, spit, and urine. You are useless to yourself and a danger to your family.

"So what is the answer? How do I survive? Well, some of it is just, plain, dumb luck. I know a lot of instructors wouldn't say that. They like to feel that their teaching can save every-one, and they want their students to feel safe and secure and capable of warding off attack. I want those things too, but I would be derelict in my duties as a your instructor if I didn't tell the whole truth.

"The truth is, every scenario is different. Some are surviv-able. Others are not. I know you didn't want to hear that, but I have to tell you that sometimes it is very difficult to survive an attack, even when you do everything right. This is especially true at close range. Anyone can get off a lucky shot from 5 feet away. You don't even have to aim, just point. And since there is no such thing as a long-distance mugging or a long-distance rape, then where does that leave us? Are we helpless victims, sheep waiting to be sheared?"

Sam paused as if waiting for an answer, but everyone remained silent. Some were taking notes, but most were just listening. Natalie was getting nervous just hearing what would happen to her during an attack on her life. She noticed that her hands were icy cold and she fought to control the shaking in her body. It was as if the air had suddenly chilled by 30 degrees and she needed a sweater.

"Of course not! NO! The answer is NO!"

Natalie jumped in her chair when Sam yelled it out. She had never heard the man raise his voice before.

"Once you decide to fight, you must do anything you can to win. Never give up, never give in, fight until the bad guy retreats or drops to the ground.

"In my NRA classes, I'm not allowed to say *Shoot to kill!* But that's a political concern, brought about by the reality that there are lily-livered, soft-hearted, milk-toast wussies out there who would prefer that you die rather than defend yourself with deadly force.

"Instead, we say: *Shoot to stop the threat.* No matter what you call it, if you repeatedly double-tap the center of exposed mass I guarantee you the threat will stop. Bottom line is this: We stop the deadly threat by causing massive tissue damage and blood loss to our attacker. If they turn and run, great! It saves us all the price of expensive premium self defense ammo. If they choose to stand and fight, well, I can live with that too.

"But once I decide to fight, my attitude has to be that of a United States Marine: *I will never lose. I will never retreat. I will win!*"

Natalie twisted in her seat uncomfortably as did several

others in the class. She was torn. On the one hand, there was a crazed killer roaming the city, but, still ... she just didn't want to kill someone, indeed, didn't even know if she could. The middle-aged woman beside Natalie timidly raised her hand. Sam, by now realizing that he may have gotten carried away, nodded to her.

"What's up, Karen?"

Karen, an overweight woman with glasses was wearing a frumpy-looking skirt that came down to her ankles. She wore an oversized sweatshirt with the words *Soccer Mom* emblazoned across the front.

"Mr. Colton, I don't know if I can kill someone. I just don't. I feel bad when I swat a mosquito. Aside from that, I'm a Christian, and Jesus tells us to turn the other cheek. As a Christian, how can I justify killing someone to save my own life?"

Sam smiled wearily. He would probably never totally understand someone who would rather die than defend themselves. He took a deep breath before responding, determined to remain patient.

"Listen folks, there are three kinds of people in this world: sheep, sheepdogs, and wolves. That's according to a friend of mine, Lt. Colonel David Grossman. Let me quote him now.

"I'm a sheepdog. I live to protect the flock and confront the wolf. If you have no capacity for violence then you are a healthy productive citizen, a sheep. If you have a capacity for violence and no empathy for your fellow citizens, then you have defined an aggressive sociopath, a wolf. But what if you have a capacity for violence, and a deep love for your fellow citizens? What do you have then? A sheepdog, a warrior, someone who is walking the hero's path. Someone who can

walk into the heart of darkness, into the universal human phobia, and walk out unscathed."

Natalie was impressed. This old man had that all memorized. He really knew his stuff. She opened her notebook and scribbled down the name *David Grossman* for later.

"Now don't get me wrong, Karen, I'm not passing judgment on you should you decide not to carry a pistol for protection, I'm simply saying that you are going to live or die based on the decisions that you make. If you choose to live like a sheep, that's okay. No problem, but you have to remember the consequences for that decision, because sheep are born and bred for one purpose and one purpose only: to be killed and to have their bodies processed into something useful by predators."

Sam paused and Karen bowed her head.

"I'm sorry, I just don't think I can do it."

And with those final words, the woman stood up, gathered her things and walked out of the classroom. Sam put his hands on his hips and lowered his head. He didn't say anything for almost a full minute. Then he forced a smile to his lips and continued on.

"What Karen just did is fine. I have no problem with it. Better to find out now than later. That's why I speak so bluntly about killing.

"But you guys are paying me to talk about my thoughts, views, and opinions on personal protection, so I'm not holding anything back. All I ask is that you listen, then analyze what I say, incorporate what makes sense to you and disregard the rest."

Natalie looked around the room. She had a question, but was waiting, hoping that someone else would ask it for her. No one did, so she slowly raised her hand. Sam nodded his head to her.

"Yes, Natalie."

"Well, I was just wondering ... you didn't really answer Karen's question."

Sam smiled softly. He liked this girl.

"Can you help me out, Natalie? Sometimes I teach like a river, I just meander around from one tangent to another."

Natalie returned his smile.

"I think what Karen was asking was how does a Christian reconcile killing when Jesus was all about love and nonviolence?"

A confused look came over Sam Colton's face.

"Jesus was all about love and nonviolence? What Bible are you reading? Do you remember when he got all pissed off and turned over the tables of the money changers in the temple? He took a whip to them and drove them out! Natalie, that was violent! If he did that today he'd be arrested for assault and battery and destruction of personal property. So from that perspective, Jesus was a criminal. Am I right?"

Natalie didn't speak for a moment. Sam's way of thinking really threw her off guard.

"Well, I suppose so. Although I've never heard it put that way before."

Sam continued on.

"And when Jesus sent out his disciples to go from town to town preaching his message of love and repentance, he ordered them to take a sword with them.

"Listen, folks, I'm no theologian, but I believe that pacifism to its extreme is sheer lunacy. Take for instance the words of Gandhi, the most famous pacifist of all.

"In June of 1946, when Gandhi was speaking with his biographer, Louis Fischer, he said.

> *"Hitler killed five million Jews. It is the greatest crime of our time. But the Jews should have offered themselves to the butcher's knife. They should have thrown themselves into the sea from cliffs."*

Fischer then asked: *"You mean the Jews should have committed collective suicide?"*

Gandhi replied: *"Yes, that would have been heroism."*

Natalie, this is just my opinion, and you have to make up your own mind, but in my view, anyone who can't see the lunacy of that mindset is crazy as well. There is no heroism in sheep. They stand on the hill and go "Baa", as they're being slaughtered. "

"Did I answer your question?"

Natalie nodded and wrote down in her pad of paper: *Buy a Bible. Find out if Jesus was violent.*

"Yes. Thank you."

Sam nodded abruptly.

"Okay then, let's move on."

But Natalie didn't hear what he said for the rest of the class. She was deep in thought. She had never expected a gun class to be so philosophical. On the one hand, the last thing she wanted to do was to kill someone, even if they were bad. On the other hand, she didn't want to die herself, or, worse yet, she didn't want her little Amethyst to be killed.

After class, she got up quickly and walked out before anyone could talk to her. Sam Colton looked at her back as she walked away. He smiled and softly shook his head from side to side. Yes, he liked her. The woman had spunk.

Chapter Six

Old Sam Colton's eyes snapped open at exactly the same time every day, just as they had ten years ago when his wife, Sandy, was still alive, just as they had 30 years ago while raising his daughter, and just as they had over 40 years ago in the jungles of Southeast Asia. Sam Colton was a creature of habit. He loved his routine, and he clung to it like the lifeline that kept him from going under.

He rolled over onto his side and looked at the digital clock. It said 5:02AM, just like it did every morning when he woke up. Sam slowly and stiffly moved to a sitting position on the bed. It was just a twin mattress on a board up off the ground, but it kept his back from complaining so much. When Sandy was alive, they'd had one of those fancy king-sized beds made out of some kind of super-advanced, space-aged foam that he hated. It hurt his back terribly, but he had never mentioned it to Sandy, because he knew how much she loved it. It was one of the many sacrifices he made for his family. For two years after her death, he'd continued to sleep on it despite the pain. Then, one morning, he'd woke up and thrown it out on the curb. He still loved her and missed her, but he was over the serious part of his grieving and it was time to move on, time to rejoin the human race.

Sam hopped nimbly to his feet. He was still wiry and strong for a man 70 years old, and he proved it yet again by dropping down and giving himself 20 Marine Corps pushups. After that he rolled over onto his back and did 40 sit-ups. Sam couldn't remember the last time his back hadn't hurt. He assumed it had been during his childhood, but that was so long ago, so distant in the past that he couldn't recall the image. More and more, everyday, Sam Colton was beginning to feel like a piece of living history.

After the sit-ups, he knelt beside his bed and prayed.

Morning God. Looks like you did it to me again. I asked you last night to kill me in my sleep and, as usual, you didn't do it. You never listen to me. You just keep on doing whatever you want, no matter what I say. You are stubborn as a mule, no disrespect intended. I guess that's why we get along so good, cuz I'm a bit headstrong myself. So, I suppose, that means you have something more planned for me, at least for today. So I'll just keep on kicking and breathing and pumping out blood until tonight, but I make no promises beyond that. One day at a time is all I'm giving you. Then again, I suppose that's all you're giving me too. I can live with that if you can. Okay, God, you know I don't like to talk much, so that's all I'm saying for now.

This is Sam Colton, your servant, roger wilco, over and out.

Sam stood stiffly to his feet, donned a pair of shorts and a t-shirt, then put on his running shoes. Last, he pushed a few buttons on his gun safe and hauled out the 357 magnum revolver. It was heavy and bulky, but felt good in his hand. Sam put on the black fanny pack that hung on his bedpost, then secured the gun inside the neoprene holster and zipped it all up.

He hated running. It hurt like hell, but he did it because he always had, because it reminded him that he was still alive, because it kept him from dying, because even though his body

33

was quickly fading away, he refused to let it happen without a fight. It was the Marine Corps in him. Once a Marine - always a Marine. Sam spoke out loud as he walked to the kitchen.

"It's not fair God. It's a dirty, rotten trick is what it is. I spend my whole life getting wise and smart, and now, just when I know enough to merit my existence, you go and let my batteries run out. It's a shame, a dirty rotten shame."

Sam opened the refrigerator and pulled out a jug of milk. He unscrewed the cap and took a big guzzle straight from the bottle. He could hear Sandy crying out to him from the grave. "Samuel Michael Colton! You pour that in a glass like a civilized man!" It was the red-cap whole milk, with lots of fat, and he drank it just to spite his doctor. Besides, there was a limit to how long he wanted to live. When his usefulness was over, he preferred to just quietly fade away.

He put the milk away and walked out to the front porch where he bent over and stretched a bit. The night was just giving way to the day critters, and he could hear two raccoons fighting in the woods beside his house. The morning was a great time for him, and he hated to miss the dawn. The birds were chirping like crazy as he walked to the end of the drive and then slowly jogged his tired, old bones out to the pavement. He wasn't supposed to be doing this either. Silly doctors. He couldn't make them happy no matter what he did. They said the exercise was good, but the pounding of the pavement was bad for his joints. Sam thought to himself: *Do they think I'm stupid? Of course it hurts my joints, but it reminds me I'm still alive. Besides, they're my joints; that's why they're called "my" joints and not "your" joints. Stop telling me how to live my life! If I want to ruin my joints I'll ruin my joints! Now get out of my head!*

Sam's mind began to drift now as he ran, slowly picking up

speed as he went. The woman, last night at class, her name was Karen and she had walked out on him. He knew she wouldn't be back. She just didn't have it in her. But it always bothered him when that happened, because deep down inside, Sam's only reason left for living was to protect his fellow man. And he was too old now to kill bad guys, to rescue fair maidens and damsels in distress, but ... he could still teach others to do it for themselves. And maybe that was even better. Not as exciting but better nonetheless.

Sam smiled involuntarily as he remembered the other woman, Natalie. There was hope for her. Something inside told him that she was special and merited extra attention.

The old man forced himself out of his daydream and looked around the street beyond the corn field. He saw a car parked off in the distance and he scrutinized it now, analyzing it, making a judgment. It was on his regular route. Sam liked his routine, but, then again, you live or die based on the decisions you make. When he came to the fork in the road, Sam turned left instead of right, just to be safe.

He heard the car start up and drive away, and an uneasy feeling reached down into the pit of his stomach. Sam reached down and touched the nylon of his fanny pack, reassured that the revolver inside was loaded and ready.

He jogged on painfully into the sunrise.

Chapter Seven

He had read all the books about serial killers, all the so-called *experts*, but they didn't know jack about murder. It was one thing to read about doing something, but quite another to actually go out and do it. And he had already killed eleven people just in the last five years alone. Many of the bodies would never be found. To most people that would probably seem ambitious, but not to him. It was all in a day's work, simply something he did as a matter of routine, like washing the dishes or taking out the trash. Although, it really was quite fascinating to read about his heroes: people like John Gacy, Jeffrey Dalmer, and Ted Bundy to name a few. They were all pioneers, part of a unique breed to be revered and emulated.

But there was one, big difference between him and all serial killers before him: they were crazy and he was not. On the contrary, he was a normal, sane, well-adjusted man. He was a productive citizen. He voted in every election. He donated to the Multiple Sclerosis Society, even though he didn't have the disease himself. He even went to church, on Easter and on Christmas. In fact, some of his most memorable chosen ones he had met while attending church. He liked Christians; they were so polite, so congenial, and ... so trusting.

One of the mistakes he'd learned from those to kill before him was their patterns. You see, it was almost as if a part of them wanted to be caught, or else why would they create a pattern, thereby giving police a string of little clues as to their identities.

But he would never be caught. He was just too smart, too careful, too meticulous, and, most importantly, he had something that other killers did not - self control. He could turn it on and turn it off. He could take it or leave it. He had the power to kill and the power to let live.

There was only one rule, one stipulation, one requirement with his killing: he had to take something wrong and make it right. He never killed good people. He never harmed the righteous and the pure. It was part of a strict code that he lived by and would never change.

He looked back down at his laptop and read the words off his latest Google search.

Otto Morriston once suggested the theory concerning the pathology of serial killers, stating that they aren't a result of inadequacy, sexual abuse, or socioeconomic status, but rather they are the result of retarded emotional development.

He looked up from the computer. He didn't like that word *retarded*. It seemed less than flattering to him.

According to Morriston's theory, the low-level emotional development causes the personalities of serial killers to fracture, so that components that are usually present, become missing. This low emotional development also attributes some common practices among serial killers, for example, some enjoy holding soft materials against their mouths (since this is the primary sensory organ of babies). This was noticed with John Wayne Gacy and Richard Otto Macek.

He involuntarily jerked the white napkin down away from his lips, then held it in front of him as if examining it. He threw it back down on the table. It wasn't that soft. He read some more.

His theory also indicates that serial killers never develop basic levels of emotional control and therefore, have feelings of inadequacy. Their feelings of humiliation and worthlessness seem to draw them to killing. The act of killing is sometimes a kind of experimentation, which is uninhibited because of the non-existent level of sympathy and empathy with the victims.

He moved his hand up to his chin and rubbed it there, deep in thought. *"Never develop basic levels of emotional control".* That was absurd. He was a serial killer and he had plenty of emotional control. After all, he controlled his brother's emotions all the time. It was easy. He would have to think about that one for a while.

After looking down at his watch, he quickly packed up his laptop, paid for his vanilla latte and then rushed out of the Starbucks. He was late, and he had to be at her apartment at precisely 11:17AM. This woman was a creature of habit and he was going to exploit her pattern at the cost of her life.

Fifteen minutes later he sat inside her bedroom closet, peering out through the partially-opened door. He watched as the two lovers kissed, gently at first, and then much harder and longer. The woman's skirt fell to the floor, followed quickly by the man's trousers. A few seconds later both people lay down on the bed and began to make love.

From inside the closet he could hear their moans of desire while through the partially opened door he watched for several minutes. This was wrong. He knew it to be so. Both of them were married to someone else. They were cheating and he knew of only one way to make it right.

He watched their naked bodies writhing on the bed in ecstasy but it didn't excite him. There was just too much anger in the way. They were hurting the people who loved them by their own selfish desires. That was their flaw, their sin, that was the wrong he had to make right. Cheaters!

He was reminded of Addie Florenson in the third grade who had kissed him on the playground, but then she had kissed Emmet Burnham the very next day, right in front of him. That was wrong of her, but he had made it right. She would never kiss another, because the very next day she'd fallen head first off the monkey bars and fractured her skull. It had been so easy. Addie had been his correction, his first kiss, his first love, his first chosen one.

He was still thinking about Morriston's theory of retarded development in serial killer's and it angered him that so many of his kind got a bad rap, were labeled as perverts and sadists. It was an unfair generalization, when, in fact, he didn't even like having sex. He'd been saving himself for years for that someone special and he'd already picked her out. She was a good woman, attractive, pleasant, quiet, and a good mommy.

Of course, he often had intercourse with his victims, but it was never imperative, never a compulsion on his part, because he had control, and sex was the quintessential lack of restraint.

Slowly, he opened the closet door and crept out with the large, meat knife in his hand. The man's back was to him, and the woman's head was turned away with her eyes closed in ecstasy. He raised the extra long butcher knife, sharp as ever, and plunged it down through the man's back, through his heart and into the woman's as well. The man's spine was severed, and he was dead instantly, but the woman opened her mouth to scream. Quickly he clamped his left hand over her lips, then, with his right hand he twisted the long, skinny knife until she stopped moving altogether.

And just before she died, he smiled and winked at her, as if to say *see, I'm normal, just like you, and I have total control of my emotions.*

Casually and coolly, he looked down at the two lovers, locked in a deadly embrace. The woman was beautiful and now that she was righteous again, she became desirable and his body wanted her. He pondered with the idea of making love to her, but, instead, he dropped his pants and raped the man without smiling. Let the profilers chew on that one for a while.

Afterwards, he sat on the wooden rocker beside the bed and sang softly to himself.

> *I looked out over Jordan, and what did I see?*
> *A coming for to carry me home!*
> *Swing low, sweet chariot, a coming*
> *for to carry me home.*

He rocked and sang, rocked and sang, rocked and sang. Then he went to the kitchen and heated up his vanilla latte for 30 seconds in the microwave. He was a creature of habit, always finding solace in the familiar. Then he made himself a tuna fish sandwich, watched the news on Fox and left unnoticed, proud of numbers twelve and thirteen. He purposely left the latte cup on the kitchen table, loaded with his fingerprints.

For a moment he pondered the thought, *Perhaps someday Morriston will write about me as well?* It was a good day to be a serial killer. Oh how he loved his work! Once again the sinners had been made righteous.

Chapter Eight

Natalie loved Saturday mornings. She always slept in, did a little reading, and played with Amethyst. They were both at the dining room table now, eating cereal, Natalie her Grape Nuts and Amethyst the frosted flakes. She envied Amethyst's ability to eat calories and fat with impunity. At 33 years old, those days were far behind her now.

"So how was your week, Mommy?"

Natalie looked up from her newspaper and frowned.

"What did you say, honey?"

The little girl put her spoon down and spoke again, this time pronouncing the words more slowly.

"I said, how was your week, Mommy?"

On the outside Natalie smiled, but in her heart she frowned. She hated their weekday lifestyle. Life was too busy and too short, especially when they asked her to work late. On those days Amethyst had to go from school to daycare and then have dinner with the babysitter and her family. She hated that immensely, and she suspected that her daughter was none too fond of it either.

"It was okay, but it would have been much better if I could have spent more time with my daughter."

Amethyst peered out from behind the picture of Tony the Tiger.

"Why do they make you work so much, Mommy? Don't they know that I need you here?"

Natalie's heart broke in two and sank down into the depths of her soul like a ship in a storm. Being a single parent was one heartbreak and guilt trip after another. It seemed like in order to provide for her daughter, the one she loved more than herself, she also had to neglect her.

"Honey, you may not understand this, but adult life is different than kid life."

"How come?"

Natalie shrugged.

"I don't know. It just is. I have to work to buy things like frosted flakes and new clothes for my sweetheart and milk and gas for the car and stuff like that."

A pouty frown moved across her daughter's face.

"I don't like stuff. I want you home with me so we can play. Just stay home with me. I'll eat oatmeal and wear old clothes from the dumpster out back. That'll do it!"

Natalie pasted on a smile and played along.

"And then I could quit my job and we could both stay home and pretend we were fairies with wings in the land of Barbietopia!"

Amethyst's whole face smiled.

"Yeah! And then we could fly across the world and sing and play with Barbie all day long!"

Natalie nodded

"Yes, we could dress up Barbie in cloth scraps and we could call her *Dumpster Barbie*!"

"Yesiree Bob. Yer darn tootin' we could. And we could have tea parties only we'd use water and just pretend it was tea since we wouldn't have no money or anything. But we could get bread crusts out of the dumpster and use them for tea and crumplets!"

Natalie put the newspaper off to her left. There was nothing important in there anyway, just a front page article on a double homicide a few blocks from her house. She could read it later. She thought to herself, *Did my daughter just say "darn tootin""*?

"Oh my! Tea and crumplets sounds like a great idea! Go get your Barbies, both of them and we can do it right now!"

Little Amethyst nodded her head and quickly jumped up. As she was running out of the room, she yelled behind her, "I get to be the blonde Barbie, cuz she's smarter than the brown-haired one!"

Natalie laughed and yelled back as she flipped a long lock of her beautiful, blonde hair over her shoulder.

"That's right, girl, and don't you ever forget it! Blondes have more fun and they're smarter than all the other girls to boot!"

Amethyst yelled from her bedroom as she opened the lid to her toybox and rummaged around.

"That's right, Mommy. You go girl!"

Her daughter came back with two Barbies and some extra clothes and they played for nearly two hours. Then they went out to McDonald's for two Happy Meals. Natalie got the cheeseburger and Amethyst ordered the chicken nuggets. They ate and talked before heading back to the apartment.

"What should we do now, sweetheart?"

Amethyst ran to the television and searched down below it until she found the movie she was looking for. She came back and handed her mother the movie called *Barbie in the Nutcracker*. Natalie looked a bit concerned but smiled on the outside.

"Are you sure you want to watch this one, honey? We've

43

watched it three times already this week."

Amethyst answered her question by running back to the television and popping it into the video player. Then she ran back a few steps and jumped headlong into Natalie's lap. Natalie smiled for real this time as she wrapped her arms around her little girl.

"I like the music, Mommy."

"Okay then, sweetheart, we'll watch it again and then we'll take a nap. Okay?"

Amethyst nodded her head and snuggled in for the next 90 minutes. The truth is, if she was honest with herself, Natalie just didn't like this movie anymore. It was about the evil mouse king who put a spell on the prince by turning him into a nut-cracker. Barbie travels the land with him and in the end they fall in love and live happily ever after. And the bitter truth was, that Natalie had all but given up on happily ever afters, especially where men were concerned. But she didn't want to ruin it for her little one, so she quietly watched the cartoon and pretended to be excited about it. Amethyst was her life now, and there would never be another man.

An hour later, before the defeat of the mouse king and the restoration of the nutcracker prince, Natalie carried her sleeping girl into her bedroom, turned on the fan for white noise and then walked back out to the dining room where her laptop was plugged in.

She sat down at the table and pulled the computer up close to her. And then she typed in the Google search bar, the question that had been nagging at her ever since the last class with Sam Colton.

Jesus Christ violence

She looked at the search results and was disappointed. The

first two were twisted sites about sadomasochism. She continued to scroll down, but found nothing of interest. She tried to modify her search.

Jesus turn the other cheek

She waited again as the computer chugged away. The internet at work was much faster, but company policy forbid her from using it for personal reasons. Her search results finally came in and she smiled. The first entry read: *Did Jesus advocate self defense?*

Leave it to Google. That's exactly what she wanted to know. She clicked on the link and waited a few seconds, all the while, cursing dial up under her breath. Then she read.

Did Jesus Christ really advocate pacifism at all costs? Or, are there certain occasions when he allows us to use violent means of self protection?

This paper will attempt to tell both sides, give the background for many of Jesus most famous Bible quotes and let you decide for yourself.

Natalie smiled. Yes, like Fox news: We report- you decide. She liked that.

Take for instance the most famous quote on pacifism that Jesus ever made "turn the other cheek". What exactly did Jesus mean by that? Are we supposed to allow people to kill us simply because they're evil? Are we never to resist, but to simply die quietly? First, let's look at the exact quote from the Bible:

"Matthew 5:38-40 Ye have heard that it hath been said, An eye for an eye, and a tooth for a tooth: But I say unto you, That ye resist not evil: but whosoever shall smite thee on thy right cheek, turn to him the other also."

*Let's first examine the strict pacifist interpretation. They
believe this is meant to be taken literally, whereas violence is
never an option. They believe Jesus' followers should indeed
follow him to the cross and die rather than resist any form of
evil.*

*Contrast that to the view of self defense advocates who claim
that it is meant to be a figurative statement. In fact, they
are quick to point out that even Jesus himself did not turn
the other cheek when he was struck by a member of the
Sanhedrin.*

Natalie thought to herself. *What's the Sanhedrin?* She
looked it up quickly in another search window. *An assembly of
Jewish judges who constituted the supreme court and legislative
body of ancient Israel.* Okay, that makes sense. So Jesus was anti-
establishment. She liked that. She went back to her first search
window.

*In this verse Jesus is sending his disciples on the road to
preach and at first glance he appears to be advising them to
buy a sword even if they first have to sell some of their cloth-
ing to do it.*

Natalie looked up and out across the dining room. She
remembered Sam Colton talking about this during class. She
wondered if the old man could be right about it. Was he a theologian as well as a shooter?

*While the pacifist would argue that Jesus used the word
"sword" only figuratively here, there is little evidence else-
where in the Bible or in the culture of the day to support that
assertion. The only logical conclusion to draw here is that yes,
Jesus did believe in the right to defend one's self against evil
in certain cases.*

What then of Jesus? Why did he not defend himself against the cross? The answer to that is almost universally accepted. Jesus, of his own admission, was sent to earth by God, his father, on a special mission. His purpose in this life was to die on the cross for the sins of the world. Therefore, to resist that evil would have been tantamount to disobedience to God and also letting all the sin of the world to go unatoned and unforgiven.

Natalie looked up from the computer again. She walked over to the counter and fixed herself a cup of tea. She thought about it for a moment. So, if Jesus believed that self defense was allowable, and he instead let himself die for others, then, he also died for her. Could that be true?

Natalie blew softly on her steaming tea. She had never been a religious person before, had never really needed it. But this, all of this, it was too much to digest in one sitting and still too much to just explain away and dismiss. She went to her bedroom and looked at the Bible she had bought at Barnes and Nobles. They had charged her an arm and a leg for the blasted thing. She assumed it cost more because it had several versions of the Bible in it. That seemed absurd to her. How many versions of the Bible could there be, and how would she know which one was right? But she liked the burgundy leather, and she picked it up now and smelled it.

She opened the book and it fell to the book of John where she read these words:

John 15:13 Greater love hath no man than this, that a man lay down his life for his friends.

Natalie thought about it for a moment. *Greater love has no man than to lay down his life for his friends.* She assumed the same applied for women as well, since she'd heard someone say that the word "man" in the Bible was a generic term for "mankind" in many instances. So, if she followed all she'd read to its logical conclusion, then defending an innocent person to the death was the supreme act of love, just like Jesus had done on the cross.

Natalie sighed. It would be so much easier if they'd had pistols in the New Testament, then they would have dealt with it then and there instead of her having to go back in time and try to sort it all out for herself..

But the truth was, despite everything she'd read for the past hour, she still didn't know if she could actually pull the trigger to save her own life. She just wasn't like Sam Colton. He was a battle-hardened Marine from the jungles of Vietnam, and she was just a single mom who sat at a desk all day defining acronyms and correcting grammar. She could never be like Sam, not even to save herself from evil.

She dropped the Bible down onto the bed.

"I'm such a disgusting wussie!"

Natalie heard Amethyst stir in the next room and walked in to take a peek at her. She loved her daughter more than herself. She knew that, and she strongly suspected that she would indeed lay down her own life for her daughter. Natalie thought about it again as she watched the rise and fall of her daughters little chest. She would die for Amethyst, but, could she kill for her?

"Hi Mommy. I think I fell asleep again."

Natalie opened the door and rushed in to lay down beside her daughter.

"Hi sweetheart. It's okay. I've been with you the whole time. You are my little darling and I love you forever!"

Amethyst looked up with her pretty, blue eyes and smiled.

"Me too Mommy. Wanna watch Barbie again?"

Natalie struggled against her disappointment. She was starting to hate Barbie, with her perfect figure, her perfect hair and skin, and the woman never seemed to age. She really was quite disgusting, even for a doll. But she pasted on her best *Mommy smile* and scooped up her daughter, carrying her back into the living room.

"What a wonderful idea, Amethyst! And we can order a pizza too!"

She placed Amethyst gently on the couch and went to the phone to place the order: double cheese, pepperoni, green olives and pineapple.

Natalie paraphrased the words of Jesus and hoped it wasn't a sin: *Greater love has no woman than to mix green olives with pineapple and to watch "Barbie in the Nutcracker" over and over and over and over ...*

Chapter Nine

-June 1st-

Good morning little brother. Did you think that silly, little lock on your desk drawer would keep me out of your diary? I think not. Sometimes it angers me that you're so naive. Did you catch the news last week and this morning? I've been very busy. Are you proud of me? I know you pretend to disapprove, but ... deep down inside, where it really counts, I know you envy me, my ability to make the wrong things right. You can never know the freedom I feel, when I do my work, when I impose, when I alleviate their suffering, when I make the sinners righteous. Did you know that Buddha says that all of life is suffering? I think he's right. You're so proud of yourself when you find a grammatical error, but your work pales in comparison to my own. You fix a mis-placed modifier. So what! I turn sin into righteousness! I take the wrong things and make them right in ways that you can never approach! You are an ant little brother!

By the way, you never come to see me anymore? Why is that? Even though you're weak and you disgust me, I still love you. After all, we are flesh and blood. We're bonded and nothing can separate us. You should get used to that and just accept me for who I am. I'm special, Mark, and you know that. I miss our talks. I have other friends, but, it's different with you and I because you're my brother and I can't talk to others about my ministry like I can with you for obvious reasons. We're blood and nothing can change that. Let's face it bro - you can pick your friends, but you're stuck with your relatives.

By the way, I think Natalie is pretty special too, just like you. I've been following her for a while, and I see nothing wrong in her. I haven't made up my mind yet for certain what I'm going to do but ... let's face it bro. She's a looker. Besides, you'll never get the guts to ask her out so why shouldn't I? You never had any guts. You live inside a lock-box of your own design.

But I have the key, little brother. I have the key. Remember when we were kids? We played so well together. It's never too late to be a kid again. It's never too late. Won't you come out and play with me? Come on out, Mark. Big brother wants to play!

Signed - Your brother

P.S. By the way, normal is dull.

Mark had to force himself to breathe again after finishing the diary entry. His brother had been here, in his cubicle over the weekend. How had he gotten past security?

He looked up at the orange cloth of the cubicle wall and shuddered. His brother, Kayne, was crazy. He knew that. But what could he possibly do about it? Just thinking about what might happen if he turned his brother into the police made his head swim. But now, Kayne was watching Natalie, the woman he loved. Would he hurt her? It was a silly question. Of course he would hurt her; that's what he did; that's what Kayne prided himself in, hurting other people. He would find something wrong with her, and then he would kill her. He liked it. He enjoyed it.

His brother was a disgusting creature, perhaps not even human, but he moved so well in society, he could talk, eat with people, even make love, talents that Mark would never be able to master. Deep inside, Mark harbored a profound love, hatred, and jealousy for his brother. Along with his feelings for Kayne, he also hated society, because they loved his brother more than they loved him. It was a cruel irony that people loved the man who was killing them and spreading terror. Despite his murderous heart, he was otherwise normal, and, despite his blood bond to him, that was something for which Mark could never forgive his brother.

Murder, yes, that was acceptable, so long as he kept it to strangers, but, it just wasn't fair! Why should Kayne be accepted as normal when everyone else spurned Mark simply because he was shy and had trouble talking. He didn't have the gift of gab, that's all it was.

Mark picked up his pen and wrote a new entry.

June 2nd,
Kayne,

You must stop reading my diary. I will not allow you to interfere in my life. And you must not follow Natalie. She belongs to me! She is mine! Do you hear me! I have chosen her! Stay away or I will take measures to keep you away. You are my brother, but there are boundaries you must not cross.

Your brother,

Mark
P.S. I am not as weak as you think!

Mark set the pen down and folded the notebook closed.

From now on he would have to take it home with him, and he would change the locks on the doors of his house again. This time his brother had gone too far. Something had to be done about him. But what?

He carefully glanced over at Natalie across the aisle but only for a second. She was eating some kind of cracker, a white one with some green dip on it. He lifted the lower-right-hand corner of his deskpad and looked at the fancy envelope to the apology letter. She must love him too or else she wouldn't care about his feelings - no one else did. She had apologized, and there was a picture, and the paper was expensive too.

Kayne was wrong. He wasn't weak. Maybe he would ask her out or something. That would show his brother how strong he really was. He was tired of competing with him.

He looked at the newspaper headline from the Gazette off to the right of his desk: "First double Murder - Killer Escalates" Yes, something had to be done. But what? How far was he willing to go to control his brother's behavior?

Mark returned the notebook to its place and went back to editing the manual on hydraulic garbage truck lifts. He liked manuals. They were predictable. They could be controlled and perfected. They served a purpose and had a very important place in his life.

Chapter Ten

It had been the end of a very long day at work, but was it really the end? All of a sudden she got that feeling again like she was being watched, like she wasn't alone. She looked around the parking lot and quickly shook it off. She was getting paranoid and extremely nervous and she couldn't seem to stop it. It was all the killings and the rapes, and then Sam's self defense class wasn't helping matters either. Everything he said just seemed to heighten her awareness that she was in danger. Natalie turned the key to her old Toyota, but all the engine did was grind for a few seconds and then click repeatedly like a machine gun.

"Darn it! What's going to happen next?"

She struck the dashboard with the palm of her right hand and then let her forehead fall to the steering wheel with a light thud. It was already 7PM and she was late picking up Amethyst from the sitter's house. She hated this company! She hated this job! She hated her life! All she wanted to do was spend time with her daughter, but it seemed like there were cosmic forces at work to prevent that from happening.

Natalie gripped the steering wheel with both hands and cried. She just wanted to go home and be with her daughter. She slumped forward with her head resting on the steering wheel for a few seconds more, watching the tears fall down onto the steering column. A funny feeling came over her and she looked up. A man was standing next to her car door, looking in, not saying anything, just looking silently. At first she was scared, but then she recognized the man as Mark, her co-worker, from across the aisle. She turned her head to the right and quickly wiped away her tears, then she turned back and rolled her window down partway.

"Hi Mark."

She waited for him to talk, but he said nothing. He looked nervous.

"My car won't start. I think the battery is dead."

Mark nodded his understanding. Then he looked up, turned his head first to the left and then to the right as if checking to see if anyone else was around. There was no one, just himself and Natalie in a deserted parking lot. Then he looked back down at her.

"I can jump you - if you want me to."

Natalie cocked her head to one side.

"Jump me?"

"Yeah, you know, with my jumper cables. My car is right here."

Natalie looked over at his beat-up Buick. It was brown with rust and dust all over it. She thought for a moment. Mark had always given her the creeps, but it was either let him help or call triple A and wait for them to get here. If Mark helped her, she'd be home with her daughter by 7:30.

"Well, okay, If you're sure it's not too much trouble."

Without another word, Mark walked to the trunk of his car and got his jumper cables. He opened his hood, attached first the black, then the red. Natalie reached down and pulled the hood release lever. It popped open. Mark set the cables on the pavement while he opened her hood. Then he attached the cables to her battery terminals and walked back to start his own car.

Natalie watched him in fascination. He was so methodical, like a robot, moving slowly and precisely, as if each movement was planned and chosen for economy's sake. His engine roared to life, but he remained inside his vehicle while her battery charged for a minute or so. Finally, Natalie turned the key and her engine turned over once, then twice, then coughed back to life. She pressed the accelerator and held it partway down to let the battery charge back up. She really needed to buy a new one, but she'd been hoping to get by for another paycheck or two.

She got that feeling again, like she was not alone and gave a start when she looked up and saw Mark standing beside her car again. He didn't say anything, he was just looking down at her, staring his 1000-yard, expressionless visual cacophony. She nodded her head.

"Thanks Mark. It started right up. I appreciate it. "

Mark turned and went up to her engine where he removed the jumper cables first from her battery and then from his. While Natalie waited, he returned the cables to his trunk and then slammed down the lid. Quietly and stiffly, he walked back over to her door and resumed his post.

Natalie thought about it for a moment. *I don't think he's going to go away*. And then she thought, *Maybe I should offer him some money*. She looked down and then picked up her purse beside her. After taking a 20-dollar bill out, she held it out the open window to him.

"Thanks Mark. That was very nice of you."

Mark looked down at the crisp paper bill as if unsure what was happening. Natalie extended it out past the glass of the window.

"Go ahead, Mark. You did a good thing. It would have cost

me a lot more than this to call a wrecker."

Mark thought about it for a moment and then slowly reached out and grasped the bill in his hand. He let his fingers touch her own for a brief second before pulling the money away. Natalie looked up and saw his eyes meet hers for the first time. She smiled and his eyes seemed to light up briefly like two children, like two little fireflies, and then the light was gone as quickly as it had come and Mark turned and walked away.

Natalie stared after him in disbelief. He was the strangest man she'd ever known. She moved her gear shift lever to drive, let off the brake and crept slowly forward. Once she turned onto the main road, she hit the gas and didn't look back.

Back in the parking lot, Mark watched her drive away until her car faded to a dot on the horizon and then disappeared. He walked around to the driver's side, opened the door and climbed inside. The door creaked noisily when he slammed it shut. Unlike Natalie, he could afford a new car. He had thousands extra in the bank. He just didn't want one.

Mark reached into his brown satchel and pulled out his notebook. He opened it and began to write an entry into his diary.

June 2nd

Natalie touched my hand. I jumped her and she gave me money. She looked at me, the way a woman looks at a man. It made my heart go fast. I wanted to say something, but I couldn't. She makes me so nervous. I think she likes me.

Going home now. Will eat fish sticks and Kraft brand macaroni and cheese. I like the seashell kind better than the little elbow shapes. I don't know why. It's a mystery to me. It's been a very good day.

Your friend,

Mark

Mark put his car into drive and then lurched forward. He turned left and coasted out of the parking lot onto the main street. The shells and cheese were waiting for him, so he drove 3 miles over the speed limit all the way home. It was a good day. She had touched him.

Chapter Eleven

"In my NRA classes, I teach my students to keep all firearms out of unauthorized hands. And unauthorized is defined as anyone you decide should not have access to your firearms. Some on the list are cut and dried: small children, burglars, anyone who you don't want to touch your gun. Think of it like you would your car. You wouldn't just toss your keys to a total stranger and let him take your new car for a spin would you?"

Sam hesitated for a moment as he gazed out across the students in his room. Natalie was 15 minutes late and it bothered him. For some reason he had taken a shine to the young women. He pushed the thought out of his mind and continued teaching.

"But let me remind you that we all live and die based on the decisions we make. So be careful when you make out your list. If it's too short, people who would otherwise protect you will be unable to do so. If it's too long? Well, let's just say that accidents can and do happen. Be careful."

Sam looked down at his training notes for a moment, but then jerked his head back up when he heard the door open.

"Natalie, so good of you to make it this evening."

The rest of the class smiled and a few chuckled out loud as Natalie walked in, towing her 6-year-old daughter behind her. Natalie's face looked both embarrassed and perturbed.

"I'm sorry, but I was just running late."

Sam's smile peeked out from beneath the sternness of his

face.

"When I said we were going to be talking about children and guns this week, I didn't mean to suggest that you had to bring a gun and a child to class with you."

Natalie sat down near the back. Amethyst sat in the desk beside her and immediately took out her crayons and coloring book. Amethyst looked up briefly and spoke.

"Don't make Mommy mad. Gramma couldn't watch me and Mommy ain't happy."

Sam's reluctant smile busted through to the surface and he laughed out loud with the rest of the class.

"That's okay we were just talking about children and guns, so it's good that you came today."

Amethyst nodded her head and then went back to her coloring book.

"I'll tell Gramma."

Natalie's face was red with embarrassment and frustration. This was one of the parts she didn't like about being a single parent.

"I'm sorry Sam. Things just didn't work out. It was either bring Amethyst along or not come at all."

Sam nodded reassuringly.

"You did the right thing, Natalie."

Sam looked back down at his notes as if collecting his thoughts.

"We were just talking about who to allow access to your firearm. For me, that's easy because I live alone. But even when I had my family, I stayed on the conservative side. There were only two people who could open my gun safe: myself and my wife. Everyone else was verboten."

Sam was surprised when Amethyst raised her hand with a

question. He hesitated a moment.

"Yes Amethyst. You have a question?"

"Don't you got a family no more?"

Sam's eyes narrowed. Natalie reached over and touched her daughter on the arm in an effort to squelch her boldness.

"Not anymore, Amethyst, at least not like I used to. My wife has been gone now for quite a few years and my daughter grew up and moved away."

Amethyst put down the green crayon and picked up the blue one.

"Yeah, I know. Sometimes people leave. Mommy says life sucks. My daddy left me right after I was borned out."

Natalie quickly moved closer to her little girl and pleaded softly in her ear.

"Please honey. Just color Mickey Mouse and don't say anything else. The adults need to talk now."

Sam waited a moment as he collected his thoughts. He nodded his head.

"I'm sorry that happened to you, Amethyst."

But the little girl was already focused on Mickey Mouse, intently coloring his ears blue and his face green. She just didn't know what color the mouse was supposed to be. For one brief moment, Sam's eyes locked with Natalie's, but she quickly turned away so Sam forced himself to continue talking.

"Our society puts a stigma on guns that really shouldn't be there. It's not good for kids to view guns as a naughty and forbidden object, because human nature will drive them to it, like a moth drawn to the flame. Kids are like that – adults are like that too! It's just human nature.

"When my daughter was still home, I allowed her to touch any of my firearms, whenever she chose, under controlled conditions. First I unloaded it, then dismantled it, showing her how to clean it. I even let her help. She was allowed to touch all the parts, even reassemble it if she wanted, as long as I was right there with her. When we were done, and her natural curiosity was satisfied, then it went back inside the safe."

Natalie began to look at Sam in a new light. She'd always just thought of him as a grumpy, old man, but it had never occurred to her that he'd once been in his prime, with a wife and daughter to raise. Suddenly, she found herself relating to him on a different level.

"Curiosity may have killed the cat, but it doesn't have to kill our children. Take away the stigma or you'll transform your gun safe into Pandora's box, and, eventually, a resilient, smart child may find a way to open it up.

"Now when it comes to smaller children, like toddlers, I take a different approach. My grandchild never touches my guns. She's just not old enough to understand the danger. Here's the approach I take with toddlers.

"Have you ever heard the saying: "Childproof your home?" Well, I don't believe in that. In fact, I believe that in many cases it can lead to unnecessary injury and perhaps even death to an innocent child. You can childproof your home all you want, but once you leave the house, that child is once again in danger. Wouldn't it be smarter to "Homeproof your child"?

"A long time ago, I read a book on Mennonite discipline, and, even though I'm not a Mennonite, I've incorporated what I learned into raising my own children. Mennonites "homeproof" their children like this:

"When the child is approximately one year of age, they place the child on their lap, facing outward. Then they place a forbidden object in front of the child, within arm's reach. As soon as the child reaches for it, they slap him lightly on the hand and say "No!". The child pulls back. They do this for 15 minutes a day, gradually going through every forbidden object in the house, until the child knows what he can touch and what he cannot.

"What does this teach your child? Boundaries, respect for authority, and accountability.

"But even though I homeproofed my daughter, I still locked up my guns. I still put those little plastic covers on my electric outlets, and I didn't leave the Skil saw plugged in. I used common sense.

"I home proofed my child so that she didn't kill herself. You can child proof your home, but that becomes meaningless when you visit friends without children. Katie bar the door and it's every man for himself, because the house is trashed! And all because you didn't properly train your children.

"When it comes specifically to guns as a forbidden object, I think the NRA's Eddie Eagle program is right on track. They take children and guns and boil it down to its most logical essence: "Stop! Don't touch! Leave the area! Tell an adult!"

"When my daughter was little she had it memorized, and I quizzed her on it often. Once a month, I took my pistol out of its holster, unloaded it, double-checked it, locked open the slide; then I lay it down on the dining room table. I then walked over to the kitchen and waited for my daughter to notice it, then I watched her. Every time - without exception - she ran up to me and scolded me, "Daddy! You left your gun on the table again!"

"I would always say, "Thank you, Sweetheart." Then I walked over and put it back in my holster where it belonged. In that way, I always felt assured that my daughter would do the right thing, even when I wasn't around."

Sam looked around the class, waiting for hands to raise up with questions, but none came.

"Are there any questions on children and guns?"

Natalie had several questions, but didn't ask them. Instead, she waited until after class, and then approached Sam after everyone else had left.

"What's up, Natalie?"

Natalie hesitated. She wasn't sure this was a good idea, but she forged on nonetheless. She was committed to it.

"Listen Sam, I have a lot of questions, and I just wondered if it might be a good idea for you to come over for dinner this Saturday. That way I could ask you all my questions without slowing down the rest of the class."

Sam raised his left hand up to his chin and felt the stubble on his wrinkled old face. He was surprised. He thought for a moment. On the one hand, his life was set; it was comfortable and simple. On the other hand ... he looked down at Amethyst who was still coloring at the desk in the back. She was cute as the dickens. Sam often wondered why his own daughter never called anymore. Perhaps she was just too busy.

Natalie waited nervously for what seemed like an hour, then Amethyst looked up from her drawing and broke the clumsy silence.

"Yup! We could play Barbies too!"

The wrinkles on Sam's face moved to form a broad smile.

"I think I would like that. I haven't played with Barbies in a very long time."

He looked up at Natalie with his tired gray eyes as he spoke.

"Tell ya what, Natalie, I haven't been able to cook for more than myself for years, how about if you both come to my house and I'll cook for you? Do you like hot and spicy?"

Natalie thought for a moment. She loved hot and spicy.

"Well, yeah. I guess we could do that. To tell you the truth I'm not much of a cook anyway."

Young Amethyst nodded her head up and down.

"Yes, it's true. But her macaroni and cheese is very good."

Sam jotted down his address on the back of his business card and then walked the two girls out to the parking lot and made sure they were safely away before getting into his own car.

It had been a long time since he'd felt like protecting someone special. He thought about his daughter and grand children far away in another state. Perhaps he should call just to say hello, to make sure they were okay?

He started up the car and drove off alone into the night.

Chapter Twelve

"You chop it up like this?"

Sam looked over at Natalie's clumsy fingers moving the knife slowly and apprehensively across the cutting board as she attempted to cut the cilantro. He smiled to himself.

"Well, I suppose you could do it that way, but it works better like this."

Sam stepped away from the stove over to Natalie's side, took the knife and in a matter of seconds the cilantro was chopped to perfection. Natalie looked over at him puzzled.

"How did you do that?"

Sam smiled mysteriously.

"It's all in the wrist, Natalie. It's easy"

"Yeah, right. Easy for you."

"All work is a process, and it's all easy if you know the steps to take."

She looked up at the cupboard in front of her as if staring into nothing. Then she smiled faintly.

"I suppose that's true. I feel very inept sometimes. I wish I knew how to do more things."

Sam moved slowly back over to the stove where the lentils were now boiling. He turned down the heat and added turmeric, salt, pepper and 3 cloves of garlic.

"You will know more things soon enough, Natalie. It just takes time. And when you're old like me, you'll know lots of things, some good, some bad, some useful, some ..."

Natalie listened as his voice trailed off somewhere into the past. She sensed his apprehension, his regret, and something that felt a lot like sadness. Then he smiled and talked as he stirred the lentils.

"That's why it sucks to be old, Natalie. I spent my whole life learning to do things, becoming as good a person as I could, and now when I'm finally becoming useful, my old body gives out on me and I can't put all this experience to good use."

Natalie smiled and began slicing the yellow onion the way Sam had showed her.

"Are you complaining, Sam?"

He grunted, then raised the spoon up allowing the lentils resting on it to cool.

"I've tried complaining before and it does no good. I regret nothing. I've had a good life."

"You make it sound like you're almost dead. It can't be that bad. How old are you?"

Sam tasted the lentils and added more salt without measuring. He never measured, and always cooked by the seat of his pants.

"Ya know, Natalie, getting old is an odd thing."

"How so?"

"Well, you see when a man gets old, he only grows old on the outside. Inside I still feel young. I remember my Marine Corps days, raising kids, loving my wife, even playing in the mill pond when I was a kid. The older I get, the closer I somehow feel to the past. My life is winding down, Natalie. I can tell that. Every morning when I get up, I feel pain. Not pain with a purpose, not pain because I did something I shouldn't have, or because I'd hurt myself, but just pain because I'm alive and pumping blood. My back hurts, my knees hurt, my hands hurt, and my ... it hurts inside too."

Natalie nodded and her fingers stopped moving with the knife. The beginning of a tear welled up in her eye and she quickly wiped it away.

"These onions are stronger than I thought."

Sam nodded.

"Yes, life has many onions."

He smiled as he stirred the lentils.

"But it has its share of grapes and apples and pears too. Like your daughter, Amethyst. She's a real peach you know? She's the cutest little girl I've seen in years. That girl's a smile on two legs. I bet she keeps you busy."

Natalie chopped another onion as she spoke.

"Yes, she does. I think she keeps me from feeling sorry for myself, for my predicament. She gives me a reason to get up in the morning. We all have aches and pains, Sam."

He put the lid back on the saucepan and turned toward her. He smiled with a twinkle in his eyes.

"Ahh, but that which does not kill me makes me stronger."

Natalie laughed out loud.

"I don't believe this. I'm here cooking Bengali cuisine with an NRA Instructor who quotes Nietzsche. You are not a typical, right-wing gun nut, Sam."

"Well now how do you know that, Natalie? I think a lot of us gun people get a bad rap in the press. We're just like everyone else. We love our kids, protect our families. We just want to live and let live, but there's this element out there who won't let us. There is evil in the world, Natalie and it must be opposed by good people."

Natalie grew quiet and moved slower.

"Always remember the words of Edmund Burke: *All that's required for evil to flourish, is that good men do nothing.*"

Natalie looked up at him and their eyes locked.

"You see, that's what I mean, Sam. You're not like other people. You're a philosopher and a Godly man. You're a good man but you carry a gun and you're willing to kill people. That seems like a paradox to me. You're not simple. You're complicated."

Sam moved his eyes down clumsily and stepped toward her to slice some potatoes.

"This dish here is more mild, made from potatoes, garlic, salt and pepper. Amethyst will probably like it better than the hot curry."

Natalie was perplexed. She'd never seen him avoid a subject before. He just always seemed to come at everything head on with no apologies or pretense.

"That's good, Sam. The potatoes will be good. Have you ever killed a man?"

Sam's slicing hands stopped moving for a moment, but then quickly started up again. He didn't answer.

"I don't think I can do it, Sam. Kill a man I mean."

Sam sighed audibly. He looked like an old, tired balloon with all the air escaping.

"Well, maybe you won't have to. You never know."

"That's not what you teach in class, Sam. You say don't think *if* I'm attacked, think *when* I'm attacked. You always choose your words carefully. I'm an English major. I deal in words for a living."

Sam gently placed the knife down on the cutting board and brushed his hands off on the front of his shirt.

"Natalie, I don't know what to tell you. If you're being

stalked, like I think you might be, judging from what you've told me earlier. Then, you may not have a choice. And if you hesitate at the moment of truth, then you'll die, and then Amethyst will have neither a mother nor a father. That's what it's all about, Natalie. That's where the rubber meets the road. It's not easy to kill; it's not supposed to be. If it is, then there's something wrong with you. But sometimes good people have to do unpleasant things just so we can come home at night to our kids."

He picked the knife back up and started slicing again, this time with more vigor than before.

"That's the way it is, Natalie. It's just the way it is. It's not pretty and it's not fun. But it has to be done. Sometimes you kill and you live, or you don't and your dead. We live or die based on decisions we make. And your daughter needs you to live."

Just then Amethyst walked into the kitchen.

"Mommy, my movie is done. Can I stay in here with you guys now."

Sam smiled and walked over and lifted her gently off the floor. His old bones creaked as he slid a chair up to the counter with his free hand and set her down on it.

"Would you like to slice some tomatoes?"

Amethyst shook her head back and forth.

"Mommy says I can't play with knifes."

"Yes, and your mommy is right. Knives are not a toy; they are tools. But if you do it properly and only while Mommy is beside you, then you won't get hurt."

He looked over at Natalie. She hesitated and then nodded her head.

"Go ahead, Sam. Show her how to do it."

For the rest of the afternoon, they cooked, ate, and then played Scrabble.

Chapter Thirteen

Natalie walked down the busy sidewalk toward the parking lot with the unexplainable feeling that she was being watched. She had felt it before, on several occasions in fact, but had always written it off as an overactive imagination. She cursed Sam Colton under her breath. The old man was making her as paranoid as he was. With a Herculean effort, she resisted the urge to turn and look behind her. She was suddenly reminded of that Mel Gibson movie about the taxi driver and the conspiracy theory. According to Sam Colton there was a rapist beneath every rock and a mugger behind every tree. She didn't want to fall into that lifestyle, that stressed-out and paranoid way of looking at the world, but, still ... another woman had been killed last week and the police were no closer to catching the man now than they were three months ago.

She turned down Ionia street and into the parking lot. Jade City was the second largest city in the state, but still had less than 200,000 people in it. The downtown area where she worked was all concrete, steel and glass, but the rest of it was mostly suburbs and urban sprawl, the kind of town most people would feel safe in and want to raise kids in. As far as she knew, this was the first serial killer to ever come to Jade City.

She chopped her steps as she entered the parking lot and glanced first to her left and then to her right. According to Sam, parking lots were the most dangerous places you could be, especially near dark. He said most attacks are extremely sudden and very violent. Natalie had parked near the pine tree in the back even though Sam had warned against such decisions. He always said "*You're going to live or die based on the decisions you make. So make good decisions.*" But she'd been late this morning and was lucky to even get this spot in the back.

She placed her hand inside her purse and wrapped it around the grip of her 38 caliber Ladysmith pistol. Sam had helped her pick it out, along with the concealed carry purse at a local gunshop. Natalie liked the purse. It was black leather with plenty of room and pockets and had a hidden compartment in the back with a holster that fit her new pistol perfectly.

Her right hand tightened around the grip as her eyes strained to peer into the thick boughs of the lone pine tree, but she was careful to keep her finger off the trigger. She had just gotten her concealed pistol license yesterday, so she was legal. But still, there was a nagging doubt in the back of her mind. Was she being silly? Was she acting like one of those right-wing fanatics? When it came right down to it, would she even be able to pull the trigger if someone attacked her? She honestly didn't know and never wanted to find out. The July heat radiated up off the pavement into her face as she thought about it.

Natalie tried to stay alert, but her mind wandered nonetheless. She knew she wasn't very good at all this personal defense stuff. Natalie just wanted to go home and be with her daughter, that's all. She found herself suddenly angry at the serial killer, the man who was running around the city, the home she'd once felt safe in, she was angry at the man for pushing her to the unbelievable point where she was willing to carry a gun. Up until 3 months ago she'd never touched a gun, much less fired one. But she had to admit, she did feel less helpless when her hand was wrapped around the grip of a 38 revolver.

Her keys were already in her left hand, so she pushed the unlock button and her headlights flashed off and on twice. Just as her hand touched the door, she felt someone grip her shoulder from behind.

Natalie whirled around with one motion, bringing the gun to bear on the center of the man's chest. She held it there with her finger poised on the trigger, ready to shoot. She backed against the car.

Slowly, she let out her breath and lowered the gun to her front.

"Darn you, Mark! Why are you following me?"

Mark swallowed hard but the lump in his throat wouldn't go down. He just stared at the gun in her right hand. Natalie followed his stare and then sheepishly tucked the pistol back into her purse. She took a quick look around to make sure no one had seen her gun.

"I'm sorry, Mark. You scared me."

Mark looked up at her and nodded dumbly the way he always did when he was around her. Then he looked down at the wet stain on the front of his pants. Natalie saw it too and gasped, but then pretended not to see it.

Mark stiffly held out his hand. Inside his palm was Natalie's cell phone.

"I found it in the elevator."

Natalie sighed and shook her head from side to side, all the while thinking, *Wow. He spoke a whole sentence.* She reached out slowly and took the phone from him.

"Thank you, Mark. I appreciate it. You could have just put it on my desk though. That would have been fine."

Mark nodded.

"Yes, I think I will next time."

He lowered his head.

"I have to go."

Natalie walked up behind him and stopped him with a touch on his back.

"Are you going to be okay, Mark?"

Marked turned halfway around and nodded his head. He looked embarrassed.

"I'll be fine."

"You sure?"

He nodded again and walked away from her.

Natalie stared after him for a moment, humiliated that she'd just pointed a gun at one of her co-workers and forced him to wet himself. She looked back at her car, at the lone pine tree, and then again at Mark's retreating silhouette. She shook her head from side to side and wondered to herself, *How did I get this way? What is happening to me?*

But, deep down inside her soul, she already knew the answer to her question. It was the terror caused by all the killings. The entire city sat coiled to strike at the tiniest provocation. She was reminded of a toy guitar she'd had as a child, how she loved to play it, and how she'd broken one of the strings by tightening it too far.

Even now, Natalie felt stretched and strained like a steel guitar string near the point of breaking. Every time she felt someone following her, everytime she watched the news of another killing, every time she overheard conversations about it in the coffee room, it was like the killer was twisting the knob on the string, ratcheting up the tension, making her scream with the newfound stress of it all.

She looked around quickly one more time and jumped into her car and locked the doors. Probably just a card of apology wouldn't quite cut it this time. As she drove away, Natalie wondered how she could ever make this one up to the poor guy.

Half a block away, Mark's brother, Kayne, watched her drive away. He took out his pad of paper and wrote down her plate number before smiling. He'd given Mark every chance and his clumsy brother had blown it time and time again.

He smiled as he watched Natalie's car fade into post-rush hour traffic. She was a beautiful woman, and now it was his turn.

Mark could not deny him now. She belonged to him.

Chapter Fourteen

S am hadn't slept much the night before. He was still thinking about Natalie and her little girl. He'd always had a soft spot for blondes, especially cute little girls with curls and bright-blue eyes. His own daughter was also a single mom, raising 3 kids on her own with no help from the deadbeat father. More than once Sam had contemplated hunting the man down and ... He let the thought slip away where it belonged. He was an old man now and should start thinking like one. That's what his friends kept telling him anyway.

He sat in the rocking chair on his porch, listening to the birds chirp off in the woods 50 yards to his right. He hated their incessant noise. Those birds never shut up! A car drove by the gravel road in front of him so he waved as a reflex action. Maybe his friends were right. Maybe he was getting old. He thought about it for a second and then spit off to his right on the woods-side of his house.

"Damn birds never shut up!"

Then he sprang out of his chair and dropped down to the worn, wooden boards and popped off 20 Marine Corps push-ups. Then he jumped back up and turned to curse the birds.

"Did you see that you blasted beasts? I'm not getting old! And if you don't shut up I just might have bluebird soup for dinner tonight!"

Sam sat back down in his rocker and smiled. Sometimes a man just has to assert himself. Then he thought about Natalie again and all she'd told him. She was being stalked. He was sure of it. He'd seen it before and knew what it felt like. There are so many crazies out there nowadays. It wasn't like when he was younger, when you could look a man in the eye, shake his hand and expect fair treatment. Now you didn't dare show your weakness or else some punk kid would exploit it.

Sam watched now as his neighbor crossed the road a quarter mile down and walked toward his driveway. Roger Cornby was a strange old geezer by any man's standards, and Sam had told him so on more than one occasion. Problem was, Roger just didn't care what other people thought about him. That, and he was a raving, out-of-control alcoholic. Aside from that, he was a pretty decent guy.

Eventually, he walked up to Sam's porch.

"Howdy Sam."

Sam nodded his presence.

"How's it goin' Roger?"

Roger was dressed in dirty, worn, bib overalls and he smelled like he hadn't bathed in weeks.

"Pretty good. Hotter-n blazes out though ain't it?"

Sam rocked back and forth.

"Yep, I suppose so. Weather's been screwed up for years though. Take a cold shower. It might cool you down some. "

Roger ignored his suggestion as he planted his left foot on the first step of the porch and then leaned on the higher knee with both palms.

"Do ya think it's that global warming stuff Al Gore's been talking about?"

Sam laughed out loud.

"No. I think it's summer and it's supposed to be hot outside. You're just getting too old to handle the extremes my friend."

Roger laughed too.

"I suppose you're right. I don't reckon none of us are gettin' any younger."

Sam wondered why Roger had walked all this way. He knew it wasn't to talk about the weather, but if he just waited long enough, he knew the old coot would eventually get to it. He liked Roger, even though he'd come back from the war a little bit touched. Sometimes Sam wondered about things like that, *what caused some people to lose it, while others could go through the same hard times and keep their sound mind.*

"So Sam, reason I came by is I wanted to tell ya that some guy was watching your house last night."

Sam leaned forward in his chair.

"Really?"

"Yup. He was parked down by the ditch there and he was watching yer house with binoculars."

"How do you know that?"

"I saw him through my huntin' scope. You know, the old Tasco I got on my deer rifle. I had the crosshairs right on the old boy. I could'a whacked him good too."

This was a backward little town and always had been, so Sam knew his neighbor was serious. Living here was kind of like being in the Appalachians about 100 years ago. But he liked it. People had a simplicity and an honesty that he really appreciated. And they looked out for each other as well.

"What kind of car was it?"

Roger thought for a minute.

"It was a blue one."

Sam smiled inside. He'd probably been drunk at the time.

"So why didn't you shoot him?"

Roger didn't miss a beat with his answer.

"I didn't want to bury him. It's just too much hassle, ya know. My back hoe's busted too and I would've had to dig the hole by hand. No way. It's just too darned hot fer that. So I let him go this time."

A smile spread across Sam Colton's face.

"You're a good neighbor Roger. I appreciate you watching over the place while I'm gone."

Roger nodded his head, acknowledging the compliment.

"So what should I do if'n he comes back? Want me to shoot him? I won't bury him though. You know that."

Sam stood up slowly and walked down the porch until he stood beside his neighbor. Then he reached up and stroked his chin as if deep in thought.

"Na! Better not, Roger. I don't want to bury him either. Just get his license plate number and I'll let the cops handle it. Sheriff may as well do something for his pay."

This time Roger laughed out loud. He didn't like the police. They were always coming on to his property bothering him for zoning violations and pulling him over while he was drinking. As far as Roger Cornby was concerned, the police were just a boil on the butt of society.

"Yeah, good thinkin', Sam. Sides, if they're out looking for this guy, then they won't be botherin' me so much. I never did like that Sheriff much."

Sam put a friendly hand on Roger's shoulder and started walking down the driveway. Roger followed.

"Just let me know if he comes back. You got my phone number, right?"

Roger nodded and continued walking to the end of the drive, then turned when he reached the gravel and headed back for home.

Sam stared out after him as he walked away, all the while thinking, wondering, *what the hell is going on*? Finally, he turned and walked back into the house. He poured himself a cup of coffee and sat down at the table to think on it for a while.

Sam Colton had never been much of a man to just sit back and let things happen to him. Halfway through his coffee, he picked up his cell phone and pressed a few buttons. The phone rang on the other end twice before picking up.

"Hank Holden Investigative services. Hank Holden speaking."

"Hey Hank, how's it going?"

The man on the other end let out with a full-bodied laugh.

"Sam you old codger, is that you?"

Sam didn't mince words.

"Hank, I need your help."

There was a moment of silence. Then Hank answered in a somber tone.

"Of course, Sam. Anything. You know that. I owe it all to you. What do you need?"

Sam thought about it, making a list in his mind.

"Is my private detective license still current?"

"Yeah, sure is. I've been taking care of it for you just hoping that you'd come back and work with me again. Is that what this is about?"

Sam sat back down and took another sip of his coffee.

"Not on the phone, Hank. When can we talk?"

§ § §

When Roger got back to his farm he sat down at the kitchen table and poured himself a hot cup of coffee. It tasted like it was three days old and he slammed the mug down hard on the wooden table top. Then he said out loud to no one in the room. "Come to think of it, I think it really is three days old."

The hunting rifle was laying there, it's dark, shiny, walnut stock glistening from the light overhead. It was nicely varnished and Roger watched for a while as the shadow of the ceiling fan blades moved quickly over the polished stock again and again and again. They had a hypnotic effect on him, and he had nothing better to do than to watch the reflection move across the wood, then disappear, then move again.

"This is quite a life you've carved out for yourself, Sergeant Cornby, R. E." Ever since Vietnam he'd referred to himself that way with rank, last name and then first and middle initials. But then, there were a lot of things Roger did now that he hadn't done before the war. He sat down at the rickety, wooden chair, reached into the pocket of his denim bibs and pulled out a pack of Camels. "I never used to smoke, but ... then again, I never used to talk to myself neither." He lit the cigarette and sucked in deeply on it. He hadn't felt connected to another human being since 1971.

Roger finished the smoke and dabbed it out savagely in the tin mason jar lid that he used as an ash tray. It was chocked full of butts and flowing over the top.

"Back in the war I could get on the radio and call in a napalm strike. I was a leader. Men followed me. When the shooting started and people died, they looked at me. They depended on me."

He lit another Camel and ran his free hand through his greasy, thinning hair. "Life had meaning." He put the cigarette down on the edge of the table with the burning end hanging over the edge. The lonely smoke curled up and was whisked away by the ceiling fan overhead.

Roger reached down and picked up his hunting rifle. He took a dirty cloth from the table and wiped it over the shiny stock. It was a good gun. His thoughts turned to Sam Colton and he smiled to himself. "Sam Colton's a good man! He was there! Sam Colton is a man to be depended on."

He threw the cloth down on the table, picked up his burning cigarette and sucked all the smoke it had to offer down into his lungs and held it there before exhaling. Then he got up, trudged over to the refrigerator and pulled out two cold beers. He popped the top on the first and drained the can in fifteen seconds. The metal crunched between his fingers and palm before he chucked it into the trash can beside the stove.

"I best practice in case that guy comes back." He reached over and picked up his rifle and the box of cartridges beside it. And then he talked to himself again. "This is my rifle, this is my gun. This one's for shooting, and this one's for fun." Roger let out a rare chuckle. He hadn't had fun since 1969.

And then as an afterthought, "And I better fix that backhoe too. No telling when I might be needing it."

Chapter Fifteen

"Now, sweetheart, let me see if I got this all straight. This guy followed you back to your car, you pulled a gun on him, and then he wet his pants?"

Natalie looked at her mother, dreading what she'd say next. She sometimes felt like her mother made light of her life, always making fun and looking for a laugh at her expense.

'Yeah, Mom, I know, it sounds crazy."

Her mother laughed out loud not even trying to control herself.

"Well now, honey, that's not even the weirdest part. The funny part is that the next day you felt so bad that you asked him out on a date!"

"Mom it's not a date! I'm just having lunch with him, that's all. It doesn't mean anything. It's just a one-time thing. Two co-workers having lunch and talking a little."

Her mom sipped her coffee before setting it back down on the table top.

"I thought you said he doesn't talk?"

Natalie nodded sheepishly.

"Well, yes, that's true. I'll probably do most of the talking. But that's not the whole point of it all."

Her mom was quick to interrupt.

"So what exactly is the point of all this. Honey, I'm sorry, but this just sounds too crazy to me."

Natalie looked out the window and rolled her eyes away

from her mother. She always hated it when the woman was right, and to make matters worse, she was almost always right.

"I couldn't help it, Mom. It's just that he's such a pitiful creature and all."

Her Mom laughed again.

"Natalie, you've got to stop picking up strays. There's no future in it. You can't date someone just because you feel sorry for them."

Natalie nodded without thinking.

"I know. I know."

She threw up her hands in exasperation.

"I don't know why I'm like this, Mom. I really don't. He doesn't even say anything. He just stands there and looks at me with those puppy dog eyes, waiting for me to say something stupid."

"Well, you didn't disappointed him this time, did you."

Natalie wagged her finger at her mother in rebuke.

"Stop it, Mom. Don't make fun of my stupidness!"

Her mother smiled, but then her face became uncharacteristically serious.

"I just worry about you, honey. That's all. I don't think they're ever going to catch this lunatic killer guy. And even after they do, another one is bound to pop up to take his place. It just seems like the world isn't like it used to be. When I was raising you, I never even had to lock my door. Now, seems like people have to carry around bazookas just to get to work on time."

She shook her head from side to side and then blew the steam off her coffee.

"I'm just a Mom, worrying about her beautiful daughter being raped and killed in a ditch somewhere, that's all. Don't mind me none."

Now it was Natalie's turn to smile.

"Okay, Mom, but I think I can handle one introverted bed-wetter, don't you?"

Her mother smiled back.

"Oh, I don't know, honey. You ever hear those news people interview the neighbors after they catch one of these whackos? They always go something like this: *He was a real good neighbor. The best. Pretty much kept to himself though. He didn't talk much at all. Really nice guy. He was the last person you'd ever expect to savagely murder and consume half the neighborhood.*"

Natalie laughed and then quickly buried her face in her open palms before letting her forehead hit the table.

"Oh, Mom. What am I going to do?"

She reached over and scratched her daughter's head before answering.

"Just go have a good time, sweetheart. You haven't been on a date in years. Who knows. Maybe he's just quiet."

Natalie lifted her head off the table and slid across until her mother wrapped her arms around her, making her feel warm and secure. Sometimes the two of them fought like cats and dogs, while, at others, they got along like best friends. Natalie thought about it as she let her mom hold her and softly stroke her hair.

Just then Amethyst walked up and climbed into Natalie's lap. Natalie put her arms around her and the three women held each other tight, feeding off the combined strength of all three generations.

Deep inside, Natalie knew that her mother was right, and she hated it. But she also knew that her mother's knowledge was a wisdom born of pain. Perhaps the thing they most had in common was their poor judge of men. Both of them had picked losers, in the case of her mother, several. Finally, at age 50, her mother had resolved herself to never try again. But she still had hopes of happiness and romance for her only daughter.

"Sweetheart?"

Natalie looked up but continued stroking Amethyst's shiny, blonde hair.

"Yes, Mom?"

Her mother was smiling like she'd never seen her smile before.

"You just go out there and find someone to make you happy, and if he turns out to be a little crazy, then we'll just deal with that when we come to it. Okay?"

Natalie nodded.

"Are you going to find a crazy person, Mommy?"

She bent down and kissed Amethyst on the top of the head.

"No way, baby. I would never bring a crazy person into your life."

Amethyst smiled.

"Thanks Mommy. I don't like crazy people. Especially the ones like in that quiet lambs movie we watched."

Her mother sat up rigidly in her chair and raised her voice at the same time pulling her hand away from Natalie.

"You let your 6-year-old daughter watch *Silence of the Lambs*!"

Natalie started to speak but was interrupted.

"How could you do that, Natalie? Are you trying to give that girl nightmares?"

"I made her close her eyes during the bad parts. It's the only way I can watch movies, Mom."

"I don't care! Don't you dare do that again!"

Natalie ran the fingers of her right hand through her long, blonde hair.

"Oh, come on, Mom. Give me a break will you? Do you have any idea how many times I watched *Barbie and the Island Princess* last week? It's driving me crazy!"

"Mommy, I thought you liked Barbie? It's our girl thing."

Her mother grinned mischievously and leaned back in her chair.

"Yes, Natalie. I thought you liked Barbie? You do like watching Barbie with your daughter, don't you?"

Natalie gave her mother her best *I'm going to get you for this* smile before giving Amethyst another warm hug.

"Of course I love Barbie, honey. You know I do. It's just that sometimes Mommy wants to see something older, that's all."

She squeezed her again.

"Don't you worry, sweetheart. Mommy will always watch Barbie with you."

And then Natalie thought sarcastically to herself: *Yes, I'll watch Barbie with you, and Care Bears, and My Little Pony, and even Veggie Tales! And then after you're sleeping I'll go in the bathroom and vomit in the toilet!*

And then Natalie's mother reached over and squeezed her hand from across the table. She looked at Natalie as she spoke, surprising her with her words and the kindness of her voice.

"Amethyst, ya know it's not fair that your Mommy gets to have all the fun with you. How about if you and I go out for ice cream and we'll make your Mommy go to one of those scary movies she likes so well. Does that sound good to you?"

Natalie looked up with hope-filled eyes and Amethyst

jumped off her mother's lap and ran to her grandmother.

"Yeah, Gramma. That would be great! Let's do it!"

As they hugged, Natalie leaned back in her chair, already relishing the few hours she would get to spend alone, not working, not caring for anyone else, just being selfish, watching a movie, eating dark chocolate Raisinettes with popcorn and Mountain Dew.

Ten minutes later, Natalie was out the door and on her way to the cinema. And, if she had enough money, she might even buy a hot dog.

Her mother watched sadly as the door closed behind her daughter's vanishing figure. She thought to herself, *It's a mom's prerogative, no, it's her duty to worry about her only daughter, especially in this day and age, what with lunatics and rapists and killers hiding all across the city, just waiting to jump out and hurt pretty girls like her Natalie.* It just wasn't like when she was a younger girl. And then she thought about some of the men she'd dated and reconsidered, *Well, maybe it was ...*

"Are we gonna get that ice cream, Gramma! I'm not gettin' no younger ya know!"

The old woman smiled down on her little grand daughter and then reached down to pick her up.

"Of course we will sweetheart! I'm ready and rearin' to go! What flavor are we going to get this time?"

Little Amethyst squealed with delight before blurting out, "Tutti-frutti!"

A mock look of surprise came over the grandmother's face, "Oh my, not the dreaded tutti-frutti?"

"Oh yes, Gramma! You know I want it!"

Gramma set her down and took the little girl by the hand as they walked to the door. Even though she would have fun with Amethyst, she couldn't help but worry about her own little girl. When would she marry? Would she be okay? Would she ever be happy?

Chapter Sixteen

Natalie sat alone in the dark movie theater, eating popcorn swimming in butter, while devouring a hot dog, dripping with mustard and onions, and watching the worst vampire movie in the history of blood letting.

"But my love, just look into my eyes and let me take care of you. Let me hold you, let me make love to you like the immortals and you will never fear or be lonely again."

She squirmed back and forth in the uncomfortable padded chair, all the while thinking unspeakable and shameless thoughts. *That is one, fine looking vampire, and he can bite my neck any darn time he wants to!*

She had the whole row to herself just the way she liked it, and she was in the fourth row back. It was perfect, movie-watching real estate. For a moment, Natalie wondered how Amethyst was doing, but she quickly forced herself to push the paranoia out of her mind. Her mother was reliable and Amethyst was fine. This was her alone time and she needed to enjoy it every chance she could.

Finally, after several minutes of ridiculous dialogue, the actress on the screen gave in and willingly bared her neck. The vampire plunged in and she swooned with painful pleasure. Natalie felt her breath suck in as she closed her eyes in a futile attempt to live vicariously through the silver screen. She opened her eyes and sighed. *Yes, for a vampire, he was quite the stud.*

After the movie, Natalie remained in her chair while the credits ran and the workers came in and picked up popcorn tubs and soda cups. These times were always bittersweet for her, relaxing and refreshing, but also revelatory, also reminding her that she was alone, that she wanted a relationship, and that no man worth his popcorn salt would have her. She had a child, and she felt like damaged goods.

As she turned to get up, she noticed the man looking in her direction from three rows back. His face was dark, and she couldn't see his eyes, but still ... something about him seemed familiar, and it gave her the creeps.

The good feeling left her as she rushed out of the theater and into the lobby. She had to go to the bathroom, but she vowed to hold it until she got home. For right now, she just wanted to get away as quickly as possible before the man followed. Natalie looked over her shoulder and saw no one. She slowed her steps. Perhaps she was just imagining things. After all, she'd just watched a horror movie.

Outside, she walked behind the building to get to her car. Normally she parked out front, but there was a string of blockbusters opening this weekend and the parking lot had been packed. Two hours ago it had still been daylight, but now, the twilight, the dampness, and the eeriness of the full moon above made her shiver involuntarily. For no particular reason she turned her head to look behind her. There was no one there.

Natalie slowed her steps some more and with one motion unzipped the secret compartment to her purse. She reached in and placed her hand on the butt of her revolver, gripping it firmly until her knuckles turned white. Consciously, she tried to run over everything that Sam Colton had taught her. She remembered the four levels of awareness: unaware, aware, alert, and alarm. Natalie felt adrenaline begin the surge through her veins and she fought desperately to suppress it. She had to stay calm. She had to think.

The shadows now somehow looked darker than normal to her as she neared her car. She glanced around furtively determined to not look like a victim. She thought to herself: *Don't look weak. Look strong. Look aware. Don't act like a sheep.* All the mantras that Sam had taught her began to flood back to the forefront of her mind all at once until her head seemed to swim in them.

Don't walk too close to that dumpster. Walk around the van with the tinted windows. Stay away from that hedge! Don't walk so ...

And then the man hit her from behind without warning, sending her face first into the pavement. Natalie's first thoughts were *I didn't even hear him coming.* There was a sharp pain in the middle of her back and Natalie tried to scream but the wind was knocked out of her and only a useless puff of air escaped her lips. At first she thought that the man had stabbed her with a knife, but then she realized that it was his knee in her back, driving down violently into her spine and pinning her helplessly to the pavement. Natalie felt her fingers still wrapped around her gun handle, but couldn't draw it from her purse. Both her arms and her purse had been in front of her and were now sandwiched between her stomach and the ground. As long as he kept weight on her back, she would be unable to draw her firearm from her purse.

The man reached around and shoved a piece of wadded-up cloth into her mouth. Natalie bit down on his finger but then was knocked senseless as he slammed his other fist into the back of her skull several times. For a moment she thought she would lose consciousness, but she fought her way back into the real world just in time to feel the metal of the scissors against her skin as the man cut through her shorts and pulled the remnants down to her knees. Then with one mighty rip, he jerked the cotton of her underpants and she felt the air hit her bare skin.

Oh my God! Help me! Save me God! I'm going to die! And for the first time in her life, she felt uncontrollable and paralyzing terror. The man on top of her moved off her back and pushed her legs apart as if she were a helpless rag doll. There was a pause, and she heard the crickets just off the pavement a few feet from her car, the labor of his breathing, and then the terrifying sound of his zipper coming down.

Natalie began to cry. She searched for inner strength and tried to recall Sam's lecture on the possible reactions to a violent encounter, but all she could see was the pavement, the darkness, and the face of her little girl, asking her to come home and play Barbie. Then, unexpectedly, the face of her little girl was like a lifeline, like an anchor that pulled her back to herself and she remembered what to do.

Suddenly, just as the man began to come down on her, Natalie's terror was replaced with rage. She lifted up her stomach, drew her firearm, quickly rolled over and fired just as the man drew back his fist to punch her again. Natalie felt the recoil as she pulled the trigger over and over again. Finally, after five shots, the firing pin hit on empty chambers with dull, metallic clicks.

Through swollen and bloody eyes, she watched as the man limped away holding his stomach as he ran. She could see the dark liquid falling from his clothes out onto the pavement. Finally, he reached the tall grass around the edge of the parking lot and he was gone, leaving her alone with nothing but the sound of traffic in the distance, crickets chirping in the weeds, and the buzzing of cicadas high up in a nearby oak tree.

With great effort, she reached up with her left hand and pulled the rag out of her mouth. Then she lay there feeling the throbbing and pounding in her head, drifting half in and half out of consciousness, totally unaware of time passing by. Finally, she heard the sound of a far-off siren moving closer, then voices, then nothing but silence and darkness as she mercifully passed out.

Chapter Seventeen

Detective Will Powers from the Jade City Police Department sat beside Natalie's bed waiting for her to regain consciousness. Will was an overweight, balding, middle-aged man, always bearing the brunt of donut jokes everywhere he went. He hated donuts, and, truth be known, he never touched the cursed little beasts. However, cherry pie and an ice-cold glass of whole milk, now, that was something he could sink his teeth into and enjoy. Problem was, he never stopped with one piece. He always ate the whole pie.

Natalie stirred for a moment and he looked over at her more closely. Even through the cuts and bruises, he could tell that she was an attractive woman. He hadn't been with a woman since ... it didn't matter. Women were behind him now, a chapter already read and not to be revisited. He was married to his job now. Actually, he'd always been married to his job and that was a good reason why his wife had left him. She had always been so clingy, wanting him to be home at night, wanting to eat dinner with him, even wanting to go out on dates. Silly girl. It's like she'd never figured out that he was a cop with a long backlist of scumbags out there waiting for him to come get them. Ruth had always been naive that way. But he didn't hold it against her, and he even still loved her in his own way, from a distance. Truth is, he kind of liked it this way. He just thought of it as a long-standing argument they'd had and she'd moved back to her mom's house until it blew over.

Of course that had been over 7 years ago.

Will pulled his mind back to the case at hand. The FBI had already been here to question her, but had left an hour ago with orders to call if she woke up. Of course, Will hated the intrusion and wouldn't call until after he'd gotten the opportunity to talk to Natalie himself. This could be his first big break on this case and he didn't want to share the glory with the feds. They always seemed to horn in on the big-profile cases just for the publicity. There was a uniformed officer outside the door, and he would stay there until they caught the man who'd attacked her. Any other cop would just go home, but Will wasn't just any other cop. He was obsessive, a workaholic, and he lived to catch the bad guy.

He'd been working on the serial murder case for the past few months, one they'd come to call the *Vanilla Killer*. But no one outside the investigation knew that this particular killer left an empty cup of vanilla latte at the scene of every murder. If his calling card was ever leaked to the press, they'd see a host of copycats and they'd never know for sure it was the same man. At least he assumed it was a man, since he sometimes left a sperm sample at each killing, usually inside the victim.

Will reached up and rubbed the back of his neck. It was almost as if a part of this guy wanted to get caught, or at least wanted to be linked to his handiwork, wanted to make sure he got credit for it. He didn't believe the guy was just stupid. To the contrary. The FBI said this guy was smart - maybe too smart for his own good. Will didn't like being taunted and played with, but, the sad truth was, they were dead-ended on this case, no further today than they'd been after the first killing many months ago. Even after his boss had invited in the FBI, they still hadn't made any headway. Will would always hold it against the Chief for bringing them into the investigation, even though he knew there was no real choice. This case was becoming a political hot potato, and next year was election time. If they hadn't caught him by then, the Mayor might as well get himself a new job. So the pressure was on.

Will shook his head from side to side. How was it possible for them to have the killer's fingerprints, a sperm sample, and even a sample of his blood and still be so far from catching him. Some of his colleagues believed the Vanilla Killer was leaving someone else's prints and DNA just to throw them off, but Will didn't believe it. This guy just flat-out knew his prints and DNA were not on file anywhere. That meant that the killer had never been in trouble with the law, never worked for the government, and had, indeed, probably lived one of the most boring and secluded lives in the city.

The secluded ones, the shy ones, they were the hardest ones to catch, because they just didn't leave a public mark. He probably lived alone, had no friends, no relationships, and no family. In fact, killing was probably the only thing he had to live for.

Will let out a sigh. At least they had something in common. This man only lived to kill, and Will only lived to catch him. It would seem that life was not without a sense of irony. He picked up his paper coffee cup but knew the moment he touched it that it was already cold. How much cold, old coffee would he drink before dying? He lifted the paper to his lips and drained the cup, then he crushed it between his fingers and palm and tossed it toward the sink across the room. He missed and it bounced down onto the floor.

After heaving another sigh, Will reached into the inside pocket of his suit jacket and pulled out the worn business card. It read: *Sam Colton - Personal Protection Consultant*

He wondered why Sam's card had been in Natalie's purse. Will knew he should have shared this with the FBI, but he hadn't. He also knew that he should call him, but he just hated Sam and didn't want to. Not that Sam was a bad guy, just that he hated him. And it bothered Will that his distaste for Sam was irrational and a part of him wondered why he disliked the man so much. After all, Sam was a retired cop, part of the brotherhood of law enforcement, had even been wounded in the line of duty and highly decorated. So, in light of all that, why did the sight of Sam Colton make Will want to puke?

He shook his head from side to side in confusion. One of the mysteries of the ages he supposed. Besides, it didn't matter. This was America and he could hate whom he wanted. But then he was reminded; *it shouldn't keep me from my job.*

After one last look at Natalie, Will got up and walked toward the door. He would leave word to be called as soon as she woke up. It was still only midnight. Perhaps Mr. Colton would enjoy a late-night visit from an old acquaintance.

Will put the card back into his pocket and nodded to the officer as he walked out. He spoke briefly to him and then went to the parking garage with a fresh cup of coffee.

Yes, he had some questions for Mr. Sam Colton.

Chapter Eighteen

Sam crouched and moved silently through the corn stalks just like he had through the jungles of Vietnam. The corn stood about waist high and was perfect cover for him as he moved toward the car parked in the field across the road from his house.

His neighbor, Roger, had called him 15 minutes ago with the news. Of course Roger had offered to shoot the man for him, but still refused to bury him.

Rather than call the police, Sam decided to check it out for himself. He wanted intel more than anything else. Who was this guy? Why was he watching him? Was he the same guy who was stalking Natalie?

Sam moved slowly from corn row to corn row, holding the 12 gauge pump shotgun in front of his chest the same way he'd held his M-16 so many years ago. Finally, when he was about 30 feet away, Sam slowed down and stopped. He watched the man for a few minutes and then slowly moved ahead again.

§ § §

Detective Powers took another drink of his coffee and then tossed the rest out the window of his car. It was already cold. He looked at the Hostess fruit pie sitting on the dash in front of him. It seemed to be calling to him, like a muse, like a seducing temptress intent on controlling his waistline.

He reached out his right hand but stopped halfway. He shouldn't. He really shouldn't. But the cherry pie called to him again. *Come on Will! Eat me! I'm here for you. I'm here only for you and I'll never, ever leave you! I am your friend!*

Detective Powers reached out and grabbed the pie and shoved it into his mouth, all the while thinking to himself, *I suppose this is why they call it a pie hole.*

He groaned in satisfaction as he slowly chewed the filling. He wondered why they didn't put more cherries in these things. After swallowing, Will brushed the crumbs onto his pants and pulled the binoculars up to his eyes. There were lights on all over the house, but no movement.

Just then, he heard a cornstalk snap behind him and immediately felt the cool steel of the gun barrel against his left ear.

"Kindly don't move sir, lest I blow your head clean off."

Will froze.

"Slowly put your hands on the steering wheel."

The adrenaline surged into his bloodstream but Will complied with the man's demand. He heard a click and was immediately blinded by the high-powered lens of a flashlight.

"Will Powers! What the hell are you doing on my property?"

It was then that Will recognized the voice of Sam Colton. Sam lowered the shotgun and laughed.

"Why are you watching my house, Will? Still sore because I got promoted and you didn't?"

Will Powers gritted his teeth and let his forehead fall down on the steering wheel. He'd been bested by Sam Colton again!

Sam stood up straight and laughed.

"You know you could have just knocked on the door and I would have let you in, Will."

Will turned his head around and sneered angrily, all the while sweat beaded up on his face out of control.

"I could arrest you right now for reckless endangerment or brandishing or a million other things!"

Sam laughed again.

"You're kidding right?"

Will forced a nervous smile on to his face.

"Do I look like I'm kidding?"

Sam put the butt end of the shotgun stock on his right toe and smiled.

"That's always been your problem, Will. You have no sense of humor. You never laugh. You take life way too seriously."

Sam knew that his smile was driving the Detective nuts, so he grinned even bigger.

"Besides, I should have you arrested for trespassing. This is my cornfield you're sitting in. And look, you've run over some stalks. That's destruction of personal property as well."

Will gripped the steering wheel even harder until his knuckles turned white.

"Guess again moron! I'm too close to the road. I'm parked in the public right-of-way. I'm legal Bozo!"

Sam leaned heavily on his shotgun barrel for a moment.

"Well, no. Actually you're not. The public right-of-way only extends out 33 feet from the center line and you're well beyond that. Shall I measure it for you, Will?"

Will turned his head and glared at Sam with true disgust in his eyes.

"How did you ever become a cop, Sam?"

"I could ask the same question of you, Will. I mean, look at you. Sneaking around at night like a peeping Tom! You ought to be ashamed of yourself. Don't you respect anyone's civil rights?"

He grunted in disregard.

"I do what I have to do to get the job done."

Sam nodded.

"Yes, I remember that."

Then Sam turned and walked away.

"Will opened the door and jumped out, yelling as he moved.

"Hey! Get back here! I've got questions for you!"

Sam kept walking but called back to him.

"You got questions, then come on into my house and we'll have some hot coffee and talk like civilized people."

Detective Powers gritted his teeth and clenched his fists.

Then out loud he said.

"Okay, now I remember why I hate him so much!"

$$\S\ \S\ \S$$

Sam blew the steam off his coffee and looked the detective straight in the face.

"Is Natalie going to be okay?"

Powers looked back at him and scowled.

"Yeah, she will, but is that all you care about, Colton?"

Sam nodded.

"What else is there to care about?"

Will set his coffee mug down with a thud on the red Formica table top.

"Well how about the man she shot for starters?"

"You mean the rapist?"

Will pointed his finger at him in rebuke.

"Don't get started on that, Sam. We don't know that she was being raped. There was no physical evidence to support that. That man is innocent until proven guilty! For all we know this guy was a jogger and your student got nervous and started firing away blindly! That's what I hate about you gun people. You think everyone should own a gun, but the problem is you don't have the training and the good judgement to use deadly force properly. Ordinary citizens shouldn't have guns! They can't be trusted!"

Sam Colton shook his head from side to side in disgust.

"I should have let Roger shoot you the other day when he had a mind to."

Will's face turned from angry to puzzled.

"Roger? Shoot me? What the blazes are you talking about?"

Sam came halfway across the table when he spoke.

"I'm talking about the other day when you were watching my house the first time that's what! You shouldn't be watching someone unless you've got just cause! You should respect the privacy of the people you serve!"

Will Powers leaned back in the cheap, wooden chair and it creaked under his weight.

"I wasn't watching you the other day. This is the first time I've ever been out here!"

Sam cocked his head to one side.

"Really? You weren't watching the house the other day?"

Will grunted.

"You think I've got nothing better to do than to spy on your sorry butt. I don't even like you, Sam. And if it wasn't business I wouldn't be here tonight."

Just then Will's cell phone rang.

"Detective Powers, what you got for me?"

Will nodded his head, then grunted several times before

closing the phone and putting it back into his pocket. He placed his hands on the table and pushed his heavy body to his feet.

"I gotta go. They just found the dead body of the attacker. He was totally bled out. Shot five times in the guts."

Sam got up with him.

"I'm coming with you."

Sam reached back into his pants pocket and pulled out his Private Investigator's badge.

"That thing don't mean crap to me, Colton! You're not a cop anymore, so deal with it!"

Sam nodded.

"I suppose that's true, but since Natalie hired my services and I still have information that you want, I suggest you take me along."

Will looked at him like a cobra staring at a mongoose.

"What information could you possibly have that I would need?"

Sam smiled and spoke as he got up.

"I know that Natalie Katrell is being stalked by the Vanilla Killer."

Will stopped in midstride.

"How did you know that name?"

Sam raised his hands and shrugged his shoulders.

"What difference does it make. I know! Okay! I know! I know everything you know, because I have more friends than you do and most of them are cops."

Will grated his teeth together again. When he found out who was talking to Sam Colton he was going to ... But Sam interrupted his thoughts.

"So do you want me to fill you in on what I know or not?"

Will said nothing, but the look on his face spoke volumes.
Sam smiled in triumph.

"Great! So who's driving? You or me?"

Will Powers moved doggedly toward the door.

"I'll drive you stupid son of a ... "

"Hey! Now is that any way to talk to your new partner?"

Will clenched his teeth and walked out the door with Sam nipping at his heels like a pit bull. Will muttered under his breath.

"I don't know who I detest more - you, or the FBI!"

Sam Colton smiled on the outside, but inside, he worried about Natalie and her little Amethyst.

Chapter Nineteen

Natalie lie in the hospital bed afraid to open her eyes. The pounding in her head would have been massive without the pain killers they'd been giving her, but thanks to the wonders of modern pharmacology, Natalie was being spared many of the painful symptoms of severe head trauma. Now, if someone could only give her a pill to ease the suffering and shame she felt inside her heart.

She kept trying to reason with herself: *He didn't do it! You weren't raped! He didn't violate you like he'd intended!*

But still ... regardless of the outcome, she felt violated to the core of her being. She couldn't even begin to imagine how she'd feel if the man had succeeded. She thought to herself *How do women survive being raped?* But then she quickly countered, *I wasn't raped. I fought back! I stopped him!* And then another voice inside yelled out to her crying in the most accusatory manner as if she'd just drowned a litter of baby kittens.

You killed a man!

But Harold Mena wasn't a baby kitten. According to the Detective he'd just gotten out of prison 3 months ago for raping a seven-year-old little girl - a girl much like her Amethyst. And that was probably the only thing that saved her sanity and kept her from self abuse.

Only now did she understand what Sam Colton had said: *When you take another human life, are you prepared to face the ridicule and judgment of society? Do your own religious and mor-*

al beliefs allow you to defend yourself using deadly force?

Natalie now knew that she wasn't prepared. She had killed a man and she still didn't know how she felt about it, about how she felt about herself. Was she a criminal? Was she a beast? Or, was it like Sam Colton had said? *You're a hero and you've done society a favor. He'll never hurt another little girl.*

In her head, she knew it was true, but, in her heart, well, that was a whole different matter. She just knew that if she'd seen the story on the 6 o'clock news, she would have cheered the woman who'd shot a serial rapist, but, this was different. This time, she was the woman. She was the killer. What was it Sam had said? "Any taking of a human life is homicide; it's either justifiable or it's not."

The County Prosecutor had ruled this as justifiable and legal, but Natalie would be beating herself up for it for a long time to come. She just couldn't help but wonder, *Did God love Harold Mena? Had God shed a tear when she'd pulled the trigger? Was God mad at her now? Was she going to hell for this?*

She felt a tear roll down from the corner of her right eye and onto her cheek. Then, she thought she felt a finger against her skin, wiping the tears away. Was that *her* hand? Was someone else touching her? She dismissed the thought attributing it to the drugs in her system. She was alone. No one was here. Even the police officer outside her door had gone home.

She felt the finger stroke her cheek again. Her eyes fluttered along with the beat of her heart. Natalie looked over at the man staring down on her, sitting in the chair beside the bed. Father Anthony Beddig smiled when he saw her open eyes.

"There, there. You'll be okay. Everything will be fine."

Natalie opened her mouth and was barely able to speak through swollen, cracked lips.

"Who ... who are you?"

His smile broadened.

"I'm Father Beddig one of the clergy here at the hospital. I just stopped by to pray for you and to see if there's anything I can do for you."

Natalie breathed a disappointed sigh.

"Sure Father. Can you make all this go away?"

Father Beddig laughed out loud softly. It was then that Natalie noticed his beautiful blue eyes. They were like oceans, and he had the longest, darkest lashes. She wondered to herself *Why couldn't God have given me those eyes and lashes?*

"No, Natalie, I'm sorry. I can't make it all go away. I wish I could. But I can't. What's done is done."

Natalie's eyes lowered and she thought for a moment, afraid to speak her next question.

"So, Father, tell me, if you can, what does God think about what I did?"

The father's smile faded away and a serious storm moved over the waters of his eyes. When he finally spoke, it was in hushed tones.

"I don't claim to know the mind of God. I'm afraid that's something you're going to have to figure out for yourself. I wish I could help you, but I can't. At least not with that one."

Natalie closed her eyes again and the tears resumed.

"Do you have a simpler question?"

Natalie's head shook slowly from side to side, as much as the tubes and bandages would allow. It was then that she noticed how young the priest seemed, like he was still in his twenties.

"I don't think I have any easy questions right now. Life seems pretty difficult."

The young priest nodded his head in agreement.

"Yes, it always seems that way. The important questions, the ones worth asking, the higher ones, never seem to have answers. It would seem that God is not without a sense of irony."

Natalie laughed meekly inside. God? Irony? She'd never thought of it that way before.

"How old are you Father? You look too young to be a priest."

His smile returned.

"I'll be 32 next month. Do I still look that young?"

She nodded and he laughed.

"Good! Maybe I'll keep my hair into old age then."

Natalie wanted to smile, but she couldn't. She feared she would never smile again. Her mood went darkly serious again.

"So what *do* you know about God?"

The corners of Father Beddig's mouth turned down slightly before he answered. For a moment he hesitated, as if weighing his answer carefully.

"I know that your daughter and your mother have been in here twice while you were sleeping. I know that they love you almost as much as God does. I know that your daughter sat by your bed and prayed out loud. She said *Jesus, please make my Mommy's headache get better so she can come back home and watch Barbie with me.*"

Natalie burst into tears and whimpered out loud like a baby. Her chest heaved up and down and Father Beddig reached down and stroked her face with both his hands.

"It's okay, Natalie. You're a mommy. It's going to be okay. God is going to heal you, and then you're going to go back home and watch Barbie with your little daughter. And you'll eat pizza with her and take her to the park to play. That is the Lord's will for your life."

Natalie finished crying, her chest stopped heaving little by little. Father Beddig caressed her face one more time, then leaned back in his chair. Finally, Natalie spoke again.

"Okay Father. I just have one more question for you."

The handsome, young priest nodded and looked at her imploringly, eager to help ease her pain. Natalie reached over and grabbed his hand on the bed.

"Will you marry me?"

Tony Beddig reared his head back and roared with laughter almost startling Natalie, but she just smiled and tightened the grip on his hand. Finally, his laughter faded and he looked down on her lovingly with a smile that melted her fears.

"I'm sorry, Natalie. I'm flattered, but I'm already married to Jesus, in a strictly theological sense, of course."

She looked down at the foot of her bed and mumbled in disgust.

"It's the story of my life. The good ones are already taken!"

He reached over and clasped both her hands in his.

"It's okay. Let's just talk to God about it for a while. He loves you and he feels your pain. Jesus wants to hear from you. He can be your very best friend, and there's no need to face this thing alone. He'll get you through it."

Natalie let out a sigh and nodded her consent.

Father Tony Beddig closed his eyes and prayed. Natalie listened, but still, all the while, she wished he was single.

Chapter Twenty

"All by myself, don't wanna be, all by myself, anymore."

Tears streamed down Mark's face as he lay on his bed in his underwear listening to the Eric Carmen song. The haunting words that had dominated his past and now his present drifted up and around him, seeming to fill every cell in his body. Mark was having a bad day. It was happening more and more often now, and he was fighting against it less. Mark sang along softly, whimpering like a child, with drool running down his chin.

"When I was young, I never needed anyone ..."

He looked down at the knife he held in his right hand. There was blood on his hands, soaking down into the quilt beneath him. When he was young? He couldn't remember being young. It was all a blur to him. All he could remember was his brother, but the memories were adult. Did he have a mother and father? He couldn't remember. The pictures in the album said he did, but he no longer recognized the faces.

"And makin' love was just for fun ..."

He couldn't make love. He was limp and lifeless. Suddenly, he thought of Natalie. Hoping, somehow wanting her to be the one to make him happy, the one chosen to bring meaning and purpose to his life. But she was in the hospital now and he hadn't seen her in days. What if she never came back?

Mark looked down to his blood-soaked underwear. Little, blue Thomas the trains circled around his groin, but they were now stained scarlet and wet. Someone had cut him again.

"It is not good for the man to be alone."

He had read that in the Bible, in Natalie's Bible, inside her apartment. Her Bible was sacred along with everything she touched. If only she would touch him. But she didn't touch him ... and the music played on without mercy.

But Mark couldn't keep up with the words through all his crying and the music went on without him. He didn't have any friends.

"No man is a failure who has friends."

Where did that come from? Was it in the Bible? He couldn't remember. There was so much fog now. What did Natalie's Bible say?

"It is not good for the man to be alone. I will make a helper for him."

The song raged on now around him, leaving him far behind, but Mark couldn't hear it anymore; it was just the backdrop for his ritual; it was the hymnal of his life.

And then Mark remembered that he had a helper. He had a friend. He had his brother. Kayne would always be there for him. He would never be alone. Kayne was a helper suitable for him. And the helper came to him and said: "Never will I leave you, never will I forsake you."

And Mark once again believed the blasphemy, because he was alone, and it was not good for him to be alone. God had made him a helper, and he was no longer responsible. But the nagging question continued to haunt him: "Am I my brother's keeper?"

It was quickly assuaged when he heard the soothing voice of Kayne: "Does my little brother want to come out and play?"

Mark hesitated one last time. He fought briefly. But he didn't want to live all by himself ... anymore.

Mark and Kayne went out to play. Somewhere, in the deep recesses of his mind, Mark heard his mother calling.

"Be home in time for dinner boys. We're having meat loaf tonight!"

It was a happy voice. He loved meat loaf, especially with baked potato smothered in real butter with sour cream. Mom always made it just the way he liked it.

Chapter Twenty-One

Natalie felt uncomfortable at her desk. It was her first day back, and people were looking at her in ways they never had before. Some seemed sympathetic, some judgemental, while still others appeared terrified of her. But almost without exception, people she had known and talked to for years avoided eye contact with her. It was almost as if they didn't know what to say. She understood this, and had even been forewarned of it from Sam as well as the Crisis Intervention Counselor who worked for the City Police Department. But knowing it would happen and experiencing it were two different matters. They both had told her that there was no shame in what she'd done, but still ... it just didn't seem good, or noble, or anything else she wanted to feel.

In reality, the past two weeks had been hell. The actual attack had been brutal and she still relived the memory every day. Sometimes she even dreamed about it, waking at night in a cold sweat. But the worst part wasn't her own violation by a rapist, she could deal with that, or at least survive it. The most painful part of the whole ordeal was having to answer her little daughter's questions, was having to watch her innocence and sense of security wash away like sand on the beach being carried away on the outgoing tide. Natalie would never forget the conversation and her unanswerable questions only a small child could ask.

"Why did he hurt you Mommy?"

"He was just a bad man, Amethyst. That's what bad men

do."

"What if he comes back, Mommy?"

"He won't come back, Amethyst, not ever again. I promise you. You are safe with Mommy."

Natalie knew from experience that innocence lost was never regained. It wasn't fair, and it angered her to think about it. What that man had taken away from her was criminal, but what he had forever stripped from her little Amethyst was beyond heinous. She would never forgive him for that, and she would never, ever be the same person she once was.

Something inside her had changed. Sam Colton had explained it to her.

"You are part of a club now, Natalie, whether you want to be or not. And it's a very exclusive club, whose membership only requires that you take a human life. Not many people can say they've done it. That makes you different than everyone else. People know that and it will scare them. Sure, some will be in awe, but most others will be terrified."

As usual, Sam had been right. Oddly enough, she felt akin to him now, because she knew that Sam also had taken not one life, but several in the line of duty. He was a police hero. And Natalie and Sam were comrades in arms.

There was also another interesting and unexpected change that had taken place inside her. Despite her wounding, despite the vulnerability she still felt as a woman, her tolerance for abuse and condescension had reached its limit. This morning when she'd first arrived her boss had called her into his office for a little chat. At first he'd been sympathetic, but she hadn't believed him sincere. Then, out of the blue, a security guard walked into his office, and requested to search her purse. At first she'd resisted, but then her boss had threatened to fire her on the spot if she didn't cooperate. She needed the job, so she relented. The guard found nothing contraband save a small pocket knife that she used for peeling apples and cutting loose thread off her clothes. They had taken the knife and it had infuriated her, but she kept her feelings inside. She needed the job to support her daughter, at least for now. But it was interesting to note that prior to the attack, she would have submitted out of fear for the man's dominance over her, but now, she was different. Instead of being intimidated by her bosses' heavy-handed methods, she now felt determined and offended. She was tired of being dominated and pressured by men. And in the back of her mind, in the deepest, darkest part, she heard someone say: *There is no need to fear what you have already killed.*

Her only consolation was that they'd never insisted on searching her person, where they would have found her .38 revolver deeply concealed in its holster. She would never be without the gun again. Never. It had saved her life and her sanity. She crossed her arms while sitting at her desk and felt the reassuring bulk underneath her left armpit. If her boss ever tried to search her she would scream and cry rape. That would fix him.

Right about now she felt a little bit like Dirty Harry and a little bit like an orphaned child. Sam had said every woman could learn a lesson from Clint Eastwood. He said it was time for women to take names and kick ass, and she was starting to understand what that meant.

She glanced over at Mark and saw him staring at her again. He was more brazen than usual and had been doing it all morning. She thought to herself, *No more lunch date for you, Mark.*

Just then an email notification flashed across her monitor. It was from her boss. She quickly checked it.

"We need you to work late tonight, Natalie. Since you were

gone so long we have fallen behind. Please plan on working overtime for the next two weeks."

Natalie's heart sank and then the newfound rage popped to the surface. It was not a request; it was an order. She wanted to strangle the pompous ass! But instead, she counted to ten, then to twenty, then thirty. Then she stormed off to the restroom to cool off in a private stall.

Six hours later at exactly 6:30, Natalie gathered up her purse, put on her coat and rushed off to the elevator. Just as the doors were closing, Mark stuck his arm in to stop it. He quickly stepped in without a word. Natalie was annoyed by the delay but tried not to show it. Mark reached over and pushed the number "1" even though it was already lit. The elevator began its turtle-like descent.

Natalie got the feeling that Mark was looking at her without appearing to look at her. Once again, the anger rose up inside her, and she heard the little voice say *"Men! Why can't I just shoot them all!"*

Suddenly and without warning, the elevator gave out a tiny screech and stopped moving down. Mark looked down at the buttons as if confused. Natalie pushed by him and pressed the button again, but it didn't respond. She pushed again and then swore under her breath.

"Haven't they fixed this thing yet? I hate this!"

Mark looked down at the ground like a guilty child who'd just done something wrong.

"Not yet."

Natalie looked over at Mark and smiled with an edge.

"You have a voice today. That's good. Usually all you do is stare at me."

118

He looked up straight at the elevator door.

"I know. Sorry."

Natalie nodded but quickly went back to pushing buttons on the wall with no result.

"It's just that ... I think ... You're beautiful."

Mark stammered and then looked over and made eye contact with her. Natalie froze in her movements. She saw something there, something she had never seen before. Mark took a step forward and faced her.

"We were supposed to have lunch today."

Natalie nodded.

"Yes, we were."

Mark's voice took on a harsh tone.

"You broke your word. We were supposed to have lunch today!"

Adrenaline surged through her veins and she quickly tried to master her growing fear.

"Well, yes, it's just that I've been through a lot of bad things lately."

She backed up against the elevator wall and smiled softly.

"I need some time."

"How much time!"

Mark's voice was louder now, and it was not a question, but more of a demand.

Natalie kept looking into his eyes, trying to place what she saw, trying to get a handle on the change in him. Just then Mark leaned toward her and placed his hand on the wall beside her, effectively hemming her in. His physical posture and presence was overbearing and her nervousness grew. She had never seen him like this before.

Just then, there was a loud clank and the elevator began to

move again. A few seconds later the door opened and with a jolt of confidence she pushed past him and rushed out into the lobby.

Mark waited in the elevator, watching her go. A jagged smile twisted across his face, and the door suddenly closed as a violent rage came over him. He punched the door and then quickly mastered his composure. He softly pressed the button titled "Open Door" before calmly exiting.

But Natalie was already gone.

Chapter Twenty-Two

Natalie had left work early today without her boss knowing. She'd never done that before, and she knew it was wrong, but on this particular day she just needed to get away from there. It had been two weeks since she'd been back to work and things were getting worse there. Still, no one talked to her, except for weird Mark, but she had managed to keep away from him quite easily so far and no repeat altercations had taken place like the one before in the elevator. He was looking at her differently now, more boldly, and where before he'd seemed shy and standoffish, now he seemed almost like a wolf on the prowl. And to think that she'd almost gone out with him to lunch. Deep inside she knew Mark was harmless, but Sam Colton had been quite interested and had asked lots of questions about her coworker, disconcerting questions like: how long have you known him, does he live alone, does he have any friends? She liked Sam, but in her heart, she believed him to be a paranoid, old coot.

She'd told Sam that too, but he'd just smiled and said, "Better safe than sorry." Whatever. It didn't really matter. He was good company and a good grandfather figure for Amethyst. Her personal protection class had long since ended, but she saw him a few times a week now, either to practice shooting or for dinner and a movie at her apartment. Once, her mother had dropped by when Sam was there and had given her the third degree, but Natalie had assured her that there was no romantic interest. They were just good friends who liked each other's company. Her mother wasn't able to accept that though and Natalie was convinced her mother was jealous. She didn't like the way her mother looked at Sam, like he was a steak dinner to be grilled and eaten with A1 sauce.

"Can I help who's next please?"

Natalie was brought back into the real world from her day-dreams and thought for a few seconds before answering.

She looked up at the board showing all the movie titles and times, bit her lower lip and then said, "One ticket for *Return of the Mummy's Curse* please."

Natalie jumped when she felt a hand touch her on the shoulder from behind.

"Better make that two, Natalie. If you don't mind?"

Natalie's body stiffened, afraid to turn around and see the face of the man who had just touched her. The man behind the ticket counter hesitated and then looked her in the eyes as if asking the question *Do you know this man?* Slowly, Natalie turned and looked slightly up until she saw the bluest eyes and longest lashes on planet Earth. A spontaneous smile spread across her face like the sun bursting from behind a cloud.

"Father Beddig! How are you? I haven't seen you since the hospital."

Tony Beddig smiled and nodded slightly. Natalie couldn't help but notice that his hand was still on her bare arm and was surprised when a tingly sensation spread instantly through her body.

"I'm doing fine. I had no idea you were a mummy's girl."

Natalie lowered her head and blushed like a schoolgirl.

"Yes, well, I have to confess, father, no pun intended, that I have a weakness for monster movies."

He nodded still smiling.

"Yes, so do I. I saw all the Freddy Kruger movies."

Natalie's eyes flashed wide and her chin dropped down.

"What! You're kidding me!"

Tony's beautiful blue eyes danced playfully.

"Actually, yes, I am kidding, Natalie."

The ticket clerk cleared his throat in an effort to get their attention.

"Excuse me, ma'am, that'll be nineteen dollars."

Natalie turned her head back to protest the outrageous price, but Tony was already holding out the money.

"Sure thing my good man, and can we also get two hot dogs, two Cokes and a medium popcorn?"

He looked over to Natalie.

"Anything else?"

Natalie hesitated before answering.

"Umm, well, I usually get some dark chocolate Raisinettes too."

Tony laughed out loud and relayed the command to the boy behind the counter who then quickly rushed off to fill the order.

"So, Natalie, do you come here often?"

Natalie just stared at him and looked him up and down a few times until he started to feel a bit self conscious.

"Is there something wrong, Natalie?"

"No, not really. I just didn't expect to ever see you again. And I certainly didn't expect to have a movie date today."

Inside, she was thinking, *this man is hot in those tight jeans and t-shirt. Why is he a priest? What a total waste of good man-flesh!* He smiled again, and she melted inside.

"I come here every Tuesday afternoon. I like the routine

and it gives me time to think. What about you?"

"Oh, me? No, this is my first time here. I usually go to a different movie theater across town, the budget one for three-fifty a ticket."

Tony nodded.

"So what brought you here today? Was it providence?"

Natalie's eyes took on a faraway look and Tony looked on with interest.

"No, I don't think so. Maybe, I guess. Who knows. I haven't been back to that other movie place since, you know, after the ..."

"Here you are sir. You can pick up the two hot dogs down by the condiments."

Natalie felt uncomfortable as Tony paid for the food. It was a lot of money and she had no idea how much priests made for a living.

"Are you sure this is okay, Tony. I mean you're already married and everything?"

The ticket-seller let out a disgusted sigh and turned to wait on the couple beside them. They both saw his reaction and started laughing out loud. Tony pulled her away by the arm down to the condiments.

"We best pick up our hot dogs and find a good seat before someone sees us and calls the Pope."

Natalie laughed even louder.

"I thought the Pope knew everything."

"No, if the Pope knew everything I would have been kicked out of the priesthood years ago."

"Really?"

"No, Natalie. That's a joke too. You'll believe just about anything, won't you?"

With that final word, they went into the darkened movie theater and sat up front in the middle. Before the movie started, they talked quietly beneath the dim glow of the giant screen. Natalie studied the priest's face, the way the shadows played across it, changing his features as the images before them on the screen went from light to dark, back to light, then to dark once more.

In her most honest heart of hearts, even though she knew it was impossible, Natalie wanted nothing more than to be held by him, to curl up into the crook of his arm and be squeezed and loved and cherished. But Tony Beddig had already made sacred vows to another, to the Creator of the Universe, and there was no competing with God.

Throughout the movie, Natalie thought to herself *You are a stupid, foolish girl!* But then he would turn to her and smile and her heart would melt like wax in his hot hands. She had fallen hopelessly in love with a priest on the very first date. Deep inside, her heart ached to touch him, knowing, all the while, that she never could, that he was forbidden fruit.

What Natalie didn't see was the way Tony Beddig looked at her when she wasn't watching. Neither did she see the softness in his eyes or the remorse and hint of regret that he pushed deep down into himself.

What neither of them saw, was the man in the last row far behind them, squirming anxiously in his chair, fidgeting with nervous tension and ... anger.

Chapter Twenty-Three

"I can't believe you were spying on me, Sam! Why did you do that?"

Seventy-year-old Sam Colton fidgeted nervously in the booth seat inside the McDonald's fast-food playroom. He couldn't believe he was being grilled like a third-rate criminal from someone barely old enough to be his daughter.

"I wasn't spying on you, Natalie!"

"What! How can you say that? Do you mean to tell me that you just happened to be watching *The Return of the Mummy's Curse* at exactly the same time, in the same theater and you just happened to see me and didn't come up and say hello?"

Sam turned sideways in his seat so he wouldn't have to look her straight in the eyes when he answered.

"For god's sake, Natalie, you were on a date with a priest! There's no way I was going to barge in on that!"

Natalie heard Amethyst yelling to her from inside the playslide. She forced a smile onto her face as she turned and waved.

"I see you, Mommy!"

Natalie called back to her.

"I see you too, honey! You're doing really good! Keep playing."

Amethyst crawled down the bright, red tube and Natalie turned back with a flushed face.

"What I do and who I date is my business and mine alone.

You are not my father, and even if you were, I'm an adult!"

Sam grunted out loud.

"Well, you couldn't prove it by me. Dating a man consecrated to God and who's taken a vow of celibacy just doesn't seem very grown up to me!"

"What! How dare you judge me, Sam Colton!"

Sam looked around nervously and motioned for her to lower her voice.

"Will you keep it down here before someone calls in the manager. I don't feel like getting kicked out of the McDonald's playroom."

Natalie didn't answer right away, because she knew he was right. She had no business dating a priest. But she'd already had this same conversation with her mother, and she wasn't about to be humiliated and chastised twice in the same day.

Sam leaned back in his seat and let out a huge breath.

"I'm sorry, Natalie. It's just that I care about you and little Amethyst, and I don't want to see either of you get hurt."

Natalie's face softened just a bit. She felt exhausted already, and it wasn't even noon.

"I'm tired, Sam. I feel all used up."

Sam smiled compassionately before he spoke.

"I know how you feel. I've been tired for years now, ever since Sandy died."

Natalie looked up for a moment and then back down again.

"Sam, have you ever read that book *Lord of the Rings*?"

Sam nodded, but she didn't seem to notice.

"There's that part in there where Bilbo is talking to Gandalf about growing old and getting tired. He said, *I feel... thin. Sort of stretched, like... butter scraped over too much bread.*"

She put her forearms down on the table and nestled her face down inside them. Sam lowered his eyes and breathed out a tired sigh.

"I guess I can relate to that, Natalie."

Natalie spoke softly back to him through quiet sobs.

"I know what I'm doing is wrong on some level or another, but I just feel powerless to stop."

Sam reached over his wrinkled right hand and placed it atop her head and softly stroked her blonde hair.

"It's just, Sam, when I'm with him, I no longer feel thin and stretched. I don't feel tired. I feel alive again!"

She raised her head up and grasped his old hand in her own and squeezed tightly.

"Can you understand that, Sam? Can you remember how that feels?"

Sam thought for a moment.

"I suppose so. I'm old, Natalie, but I'm not dead, at least not yet. I remember."

"Hey Mommy! Can I have some more chicken nuggets?"

Sam and Natalie were so engrossed in their conversation, that neither of them had seen Amethyst walk up. Natalie looked over to her daughter and pasted back on her best mommy smile.

"Mommy, your eyes are all wet."

Still smiling, Natalie let go of Sam's hand and pulled Amethyst up on to her lap. She hugged her and planted an affectionate kiss on the little girl's forehead.

"I think there's too much onions in my cheeseburger again, honey. You know how those onions make Mommy cry."

Amethyst smiled.

"Yup. I know. Those onions are nasty little boogers! I don't like 'em neither! I'm just like you. Must be herited."

With that, Sam placed the palms of his hands on the table and lifted himself up slowly.

"Oh, man do I feel old today."

His ankles cracked loudly and Amethyst laughed.

"Sam! Your body is falling apart!"

He bent over and kissed the little girl on the top of the head.

"More than you know, Amethyst. More than you know. Now if you young ladies will excuse me, I've got a hot date!"

Sam winked at Natalie and turned to walk out the door. Natalie smiled as he left.

"What's a hot date, Mommy?"

Natalie's face took on her tired look again.

"Well, honey. It's hard to explain in little-girl terms. I guess it's kind of like when your Barbie doll gets a new Ken doll and they just can't wait to play with each other."

Amethyst's eyes brightened.

"Oh, that sounds like fun!"

Then she took her mother's face between her soft, babylike hands and turned Natalie so she was looking her straight in the face.

"Mommy, let's you and I go have a hot date!"

Natalie smiled and began tickling her little girl under the arms and Amethyst squealed with delight.

"Good idea, sweetheart! Let's go play!"

Chapter Twenty-Four

"It's just that she's so beautiful! And when Natalie smiles her whole face lights up. And she's been through so much and I love to talk to her. I love it when she talks about her daughter, Amethyst. She's such a cute little girl. I met her once in the hospital and then once at their apartment. She sat beside me and we watched a movie called "Barbietopia" while eating a frozen pizza. She snuggled into my side and I put my arm around her."

Father Tony Beddig looked up but his friend didn't answer him so he went on.

"Is that what I'm missing by being a priest? Is that what it's like to be a father, a real father I mean and not something made up by the church? And then Amethyst went to bed and I got to tuck her in and pray with her. It was wonderful the way she talks, like you're really there, and whatever is on her mind she just blurts it out and it's so funny sometimes that I have to laugh just thinking about it.

"But the best part was going back to the couch with Natalie and just holding her. Don't worry, all we did is talk. Well ... I guess we did a little more than talk but ... I'm only human!"

Tony squirmed on his knees and shifted his elbows to a different position on the bed.

"If you want to know the truth, Lord, I just wanted to take her right there on the couch with Amethyst in the next room! I wanted to grab her and kiss her and touch her all over and then carry her into the bedroom and ..."

A tear crept down the right side of his face, but he quickly moved his hand up to wipe it away.

"It's not just the sex part, God. It's the closeness. It's the physical touch that I miss. I think I need it. And I think you made me this way, to need another person I mean. It's different with her than it is with you. Sure, you're my father and my friend, and I talk to you more than anyone but ... you never answer me!"

The volume of Tony's voice started to rise but he quickly caught himself and lowered his tone.

"It's just ... I talk to you everyday and you never say anything! And ... you never hold me. I think I need that, God. I think I need to be held, to be touched. I need to reach out, and to touch. And when I can't do it, it leaves an awfully big hole inside me."

Tony opened his eyes and looked up at the wooden cross on his wall. Tears were streaming down his face again, but this time he made no effort to stop them.

"Why? Why can't I be with her and with you?"

Tony was yelling now without realizing it, but still ... God did not answer him. Tony climbed off his knees and up onto the simple bed. He grabbed his pillow and pulled it in close to his face. He wept bitterly into its cloth, smothering his moans and wails so that no one else could hear. He reached up and pulled at the white collar around his neck until it came free and fell to the blanket beside him.

He looked over at the phone on the nightstand beside his bed and yearned to pick it up, to call, to reach out and to touch. Natalie would be at work right now, and if he called she would answer and her voice would perk up when he spoke to her.

He looked back up at the cross and pleaded.

"It is not good for man to be alone. You said that. It's in the Bible. You said it wasn't good for me to be like this. You made woman to be a partner for me. So why would you tell me I can't fulfill my natural desires, feelings that you put inside me?"

And then a queasiness hit him in the pit of his stomach and he wanted to vomit with the realization. *I didn't ask you to be this way. You had a choice. You made the vow of your own free will.*

"What did you say?"

Tony listened, but there was no answer.

"God? Is that you? Is that your voice?"

There was the sound of a construction crew working down the street, repairing potholes in the road. The clock beside his bed ticked loudly, each tick a boom that blasted his heart and tore at his resolve.

Still, he listened. The ticking grew louder and the construction sounds grew faint until he could no longer hear them.

"Yes, God. I know. I did make the choice. It was my decision. But still ... I think maybe ... I made a ..."

At that moment, a black, tiger-striped cat jumped up onto his bed and slowly walked up and nuzzled his tear-stained face. Tony reached over instinctively and touched the big cat. Immediately it began to purr loudly.

"Where did you come from? I've never seen you before. How did you get in here?"

Tony rolled over onto his back and the cat walked up bravely, worked his paws up and down on his chest, the claws digging in and letting go with each movement. Tony winced in pain several times, but made no move to stop the cat.

Finally, the cat lay down on his chest and settled in. Tony

felt the warmth merging with his own, felt the rise and fall of his chest and heard the gentle purring of the cat, like a tiny, little engine of flesh and blood and bone. The cat lowered his head and gently closed his eyes and fell fast asleep as if he owned the priest and all his time.

Tony reached up his right hand and pet the cat softly, relishing the feel of the fur and the sound of his breathing. To reach out, to touch.

A verse from the Bible ran through his head and he quoted it from memory as he often did.

Remember your word to your servant,
for you have given me hope.
My comfort in my suffering is this:
Your promise preserves my life.

"I know, God. I made you a promise. It's just that I have a feeling that I shouldn't have made it. Please be patient with your servant. I still love you, and I still want to do your will. I just think I might have made a mistake. But I'll do what you want. Don't I always? In the end I mean."

Tony glanced up at the cross and then over at the telephone, then back down at the cat.

"So why do I have to choose, Lord? I know, I know! I made a vow, a sacred vow, a stupid, sacred vow!" Then he looked back down at the cat.

"I think I'll name you Comfort."

Tony then closed his eyes and felt the tension leave. He felt the warm and fuzzy cat on his chest and his own breathing gradually slowed and became deeper and deeper.

And in the throes of his sleep, he found comfort.

Chapter Twenty-Five

"You look awful happy today, Tony. What are you thinking about?"

Tony Beddig sat at the kitchen table across from Natalie, just looking at her with a smile on his face. He looked down at his plate and pushed around a few elbows of macaroni and cheese.

"Oh, I'm just so pleased that you cook so well."

Natalie blushed.

"For god's sake, Tony, it's just macaroni and cheese from the box."

His blue eyes looked up at her and smiled. "That's true, but it's the best boxed macaroni and cheese that I've ever had. And these hot dogs are great!"

"You sound like a man who's not thinking clearly, Tony."

He shook his head in disagreement.

"On the contrary, I don't think I've ever felt more clearly about things in my life."

Natalie lay down her fork and tightened her brow when she looked at him.

"What things are you talking about?"

"Oh, nothing in particular, at least not anything I can talk about today." He hesitated. "Ask me again tomorrow."

Natalie raised her brows and her pulse quickened.

"Tomorrow? What's so special about tomorrow?"

Tony turned away and smiled mischievously.

"You'll find out. Just be patient."

"You little snot! You can't bring something up like that and then tell me to wait until tomorrow. You have to tell me now!"

He took another bite of his macaroni and cheese and then cut off another piece of hot dog with the side of his fork.

"Don't rush me, woman. All good things come to those who wait."

"Ahh! You are a terrible man!" She jumped off her chair and rushed over towards him. Tony responded by jumping up and running into the living room with Natalie close on his heels. She caught him at the couch and they both landed in a heap on the carpet.

"That is so terrible! Why do you always tease me like that?"

Natalie was on top of him now, pressing down against the full length of his body. She felt the heat rise up from him and saw the redness in his cheeks. He reached up and wrapped his arms around her. She responded by lowering her face down to his. They kissed.

"We shouldn't do this, Natalie."

She sensed no conviction in his voice.

"I know."

They kissed again.

"We should stop right now, Natalie."

She returned his words with a deeper kiss than before.

"Yes, we will. We'll stop right now."

Natalie could feel his desire for her growing, and it took away what was left of her restraint. Tony replied desperately.

"Let's stop right now!"

"Yes, we'll stop!"

Natalie pressed her body up against his own, reached down and took his face in her palms and kissed him long and slow. Tony responded to her kiss by placing his hands to her jeans and squeezing hard and pressing down.

"But Amethyst?"

Natalie kissed him again.

"She's asleep."

Tony hesitated one last time before rolling over and pinning Natalie to the carpet. He had but one last thought before completely giving in to his passion.

"*Forgive me, Father.*"

As the two, young lovers were swept out to sea by an irresistible wave ... the shoreline disappeared.

Chapter Twenty-Six

"Forgive you, Father, for you have sinned."

Father Tony Beddig perked up when he heard the beginning of his next confession. He didn't recognize the voice as belonging to one of his regular parishioners. And what was that smell?

"Excuse me? What did you say?"

The voice came back at him like a sledge hammer.

"I said, Forgive you, Father, for you have sinned!"

Tony's brow furled as he squinted his eyes, trying to see past the screen into the booth beside him. Tony chuckled nervously to himself before answering. It was a sweet smell but he couldn't quite place it.

"I think you said that wrong. Don't you mean forgive *me* father for *I* have sinned?"

Tony heard only silence from the booth next door as the man shook his head back and forth. Finally...

"Isn't it still a sin for a priest to break his holy vows before the Lord?"

Ice-cold guilt rushed into Tony's body as his fingers became numb and began to tingle.

"Why? Are you a priest?"

"No, I'm not. But you are and you have cheated on God."

The adrenaline was coursing through Father Beddig's veins now making his nervousness uncontrollable. Finally, he found the courage to speak.

"What do you mean?"

A single word came booming back at him, nailing him to the wooden seat of the confession booth.

"Natalie!"

Tony's heart froze in his chest and his hands began to shake. Who was this man? How did he know about Natalie? He stuttered back a lame denial.

"I ... I don't know what you're talking about. Who are you?"

The man laughed, causing Tony to cringe back into the chair. It was inhuman laughter, filled with malice and rage.

"Uh ohhh! Now that's two sins, father. I'm not even a Catholic, and I know there's been a lot of changes in the church lately, but ... I'm pretty sure lying is still a sin."

Tony remained silent, his mind racing, wondering what to do, what to say. The man's voice was eerie and taunting at the same time.

"Would *you* like to confess to *me*, father?"

Tony was silent for a moment, filled with a mixture of feelings: anger, regret, shame, and remorse. When he finally found his voice, it was forced and took on an artificial sense of authority.

"No. I am the priest and I have nothing to confess. So either confess your sins before God or leave the sanctity of the confession booth!"

There was a momentary silence and then Tony heard the rustle of fabric and what sounded like a zipper opening up.

"Well, I guess I do have one sin to confess."

Tony's mind was racing now, trying to figure out how to get himself out of this predicament.

"Okay then. I will hear your confession."

The man laughed softly and a tingle ran down Tony's spine. Tony started to get up but hesitated upon hearing the man's parting words.

"Forgive me, father, for I am about to sin."

Tony heard a metallic sound and then felt something hard hit his forehead, pushing him back ever so slightly. Then something ran down the bridge of his nose, so he reached up to wipe it away. His hand came down and he saw the blood on his fingertips. A wave of nausea swept over him, and as his eyes closed and his time on this earth faded to black, Tony recognized the distinct smell of vanilla.

§ § §

Detective Will Powers sat at his desk nursing a glass of ice-cold whole milk and chewing on the rest of his Hostess Apple pie. He stared at the picture of Father Tony Beddig's dead body and sighed. First, he'd been chewed out by his boss for withholding evidence from the FBI, then they'd been out of cherry pies at the Seven-Eleven, and now a priest was dead. Will shook his head in disgust. This day was going from bad to worse.

He'd been at the crime scene, read the coroner's report, even interviewed people at the scene, but they still weren't any closer to catching the killer than they were before. The FBI acted like they knew what was going on, but Will knew better. They didn't have a clue either. Will was a little confused. It was definitely the work of the Vanilla Killer, but this murder just didn't match his pattern. The fingerprints on the latte cup matched those of the other crime scenes, but this crime was different. This was more like a professional hit than a serial killing.

"Good morning, partner!"

Startled, Will looked up and swung his feet down off the extra chair that they were propped on. Sam Colton smiled from ear to ear.

"Why thanks, Will. Don't mind if I do. I'll just have a seat right here."

Will growled under his breath as he spoke.

"What are you doing in here, Colton? This room is off limits to civilians! So get the hell out of here before I have you tossed out!"

Sam Colton's old eyes opened even wider as he pulled out his wallet and showed Will his new badge.

"I already told you once that tin, Private Eye badge don't mean crap to me, so just put it away and get out of my space!"

Sam leaned a little closer and extended the badge out to him.

"Look closer, Will. I'm your new partner! Isn't that exciting?"

Will leaned forward to get a closer look and his eyes popped open wide with fury.

"This is a Special Officer's badge! Where did you get it?"

Sam reached into his shirt pocket, pulled out a letter and plopped it on Will's cluttered desk. Detective Powers picked it up and read it quickly, his face growing redder and redder by the second.

"Careful, Will, we don't want one of those clogged arteries to blow up on you from all the self-induced stress. The Chief just thought you could use a little help. This is a tough case."

Will dropped the letter onto the desk, leaned forward and ran his fingers through his greasy, gray hair.

"The Chief deputized you and made you my partner? For Pete's sake you must be 189 years old! Can you even shoot a gun anymore?"

Without another word, Sam surprised him by jumping off his chair, dropping down onto the floor and pumping out 20 Marine Corps pushups. Upon finishing, he sat back down in his chair, crossed his right leg over his left and leaned back. Will couldn't help but notice Sam wasn't even breathing heavy.

"Actually, Will, I'll be 71 in September, and you darn well know I can shoot the grin off a perp's face at 75 yards!"

Will sighed and slumped back in his chair. Yep! This day was going from bad to worse! For a moment he considered early retirement. He had enough years in. Maybe his wife was still around? But he quickly shrugged the idea off. He lived to get the bad guy, and he wanted this Vanilla Killer more than anything ... even if he had to work with Sam Colton to do it.

§ § §

Natalie sat with her morning coffee in the break room at work all alone. But she was happy. She'd been spending a lot of time with Tony, and he was such an amazing man. He was warm, and kind, and generous. True, most of their time had been spent over the phone, but the conversations had been divine! She reached up to rub her tired eyes. Natalie had done her best to cover the dark circles this morning as staying up late and talking to him on the phone had become a habit, one that she was becoming addicted to. She wasn't worried, there would be plenty of time to sleep after she died. Although, she wondered why he hadn't called her last night.

But then ... there were complications. There always were. Complexity seemed to follow her, dog her, hunt her down like a wolf and pounce on her at every turn. As Sam had so gently put it "He's a priest! You can't marry him!" That's when she'd bared her female fangs and hissed at him like a cat. "What do you know! You're just an old man!"

She'd regretted the words the moment they'd been uttered, but words, like bullets, could never be retrieved. That was two days ago and they hadn't spoken since. But Natalie didn't care. She was lost in love and that's all she cared about. She didn't want anyone messing up her romantic high. After all, these feelings come so few and far between. Times like these had to be savored, and Sam Colton just didn't understand. How could he? He was a man.

Natalie looked over the rim of her tea cup and saw those eyes from across the room staring at her again. Mark had become bold and blatant. Something inside her told her to be careful, but she was in love and not about to let anything or anyone get in the way of her feelings. They were just too important to her.

The woman two chairs down finished reading her newspaper and plunked it down on the table as she got up and walked away. Natalie looked at it in passing and her heart froze in her chest.

There, on the front page, was a picture of the man she loved. The headline read: "Local Priest Murdered in Confession Booth".

Natalie's fingers went limp and her tea cup slipped through them and landed on the table in front of her, splashing up and onto her blouse. The brown tea soaked in and spread across the cotton, leaching into the fabric, spreading, growing, staining her heart and every fiber of her life. Tears formed and spread, but she quickly wiped them away as she got up and walked out of the break room.

Mark's eyes followed her figure as she left the room. She was a very attractive woman and he loved her with all his heart. His mouth opened slightly and he frowned. She had almost belonged to him. Soon. She had been his chosen. But now ... she had ruined it all. Her and the priest.

Mark looked down at the newspaper in front of him and read to himself.

"The execution style murder took place early in the afternoon when the church was empty, oddly enough, in the confession booth. When asked if this was related to the recent serial killings, Detective Will Powers of the City Police Department declined to comment."

This had been his first murder. True, his brother, Kayne, had helped him and even walked him through it, but the killing belonged to him. And now, he would make one, final plea to Natalie. And if she refused to come to her senses ... well, then, let Kayne have his way. After all, he was not his brother's keeper.

Chapter Twenty-Seven

Mark typed away furiously on his laptop keyboard, pausing every few sentences to sip his Starbucks Mocha Latte. He didn't usually instant message, but Kayne had been on line and he wanted to talk about this right away. It was important.

> *Mark: But there has to be a way to save her!*
> *Kayne: If there is then I don't see it. She betrayed you! Can't you see that!*
> *Mark: You don't know that for sure!*
> *Kayne: Open your eyes little brother! She was screwing the priest.*
> *Mark: You don't know that! You can't prove it!*
> *Kayne: Denial!*
> *Mark: Shut up!*
> *Kayne: Double denial!*

Mark paused and ran his nervous fingers through his hair. He gritted his teeth and went back to typing.

> *Mark: It would be out of character for her to act in a selfish and unrighteous manner. She lives her life for her daughter. It's not logical for her to screw the priest.*
> *Kayne: He's a priest, sworn to celibacy, but he screwed her. Priests do that all the time. You read the news! They even do it to little boys! He broke his vows to God. He sinned against God and you were right to kill him. Why is it any different for Natalie? Because you love her? You have to be consistent in dealing out justice or it's not really justice.*

Mark: But I have no proof. Justice demands evidence.
Kayne: You saw them on the couch.
Mark: They were just watching TV.
Kayne: His arm was around her.
Kayne: Her head was on his shoulder.

Mark sipped his mocha and burned his tongue.

Kayne: They kissed. You saw. She liked it.
Kayne: He squeezed her breast.
Kayne: She touched his ...

"Stop it! Just shut up!"

It took a moment for Mark to realize he'd just shouted out loud in Starbucks. He looked up and people were staring at him over their newspapers and laptops. Mark looked back down and went back to typing.

Mark: I know. I saw it too.
Kayne: You have a picture.

Mark nodded but typed nothing. A message popped up in another window "*You have mail from Kayne*". He went to his email and pulled up the message. Embedded in the body was a picture of Natalie and Tony Beddig laying on the couch, his face was covering hers, her hand was on his rump, her fingernails digging in to his jeans in a tight embrace. A tear ran down Mark's face, but he quickly wiped it away. His fingers paused over the keyboard, but then, finally, he typed.

Mark: I know.
Kayne: I'm sorry. At one time she was special.
Mark: She was my chosen one.
Kayne: Yes, chosen, consecrated to a special purpose.
Mark: Do I have to do it?
Kayne: Sin demands payment.
Mark: Yes. I know. Give me time.

Kayne: How much time do you need?
Mark: Not much.
Kayne: Good bye my brother.
Mark: Good bye my brother.

Mark exited the program and closed his laptop. The mocha had cooled somewhat and he took a larger sip. Already his mind was working faster and faster and faster. A plan took shape, festered in his mind and came to fruition.

The elevator ... yes ... the elevator.

Chapter Twenty-Eight

"Natalie Katrell is the key to cracking this case. You don't have to find the Vanilla Killer. Just put Natalie under surveillance and the killer will come to you."

Will Powers finished chewing the last bite of his Hostess cherry pie before answering.

"Hmmm, so let me see if I got this straight. You want me to go in there and tell the Chief that in order to catch the most vicious serial killer in the state, I'm going to wait until he comes to me?" Will washed his pie down with a drink of whole milk. "Are you out of your mind, Colton? I want to keep my job!"

Sam Colton's lean and wiry frame shifted back and forth in the chair in front of Will's desk.

"Well, I don't know as I'd word it exactly like that. But you get the general idea. I tell you, Will, this guy has a thing for Natalie and he's not going to stop until he's played out whatever plan he has in mind."

Will Powers brushed the crumbs off his white shirt and they fell to the dirty, green tile floor beneath his desk.

"Evidence, Colton, I need evidence! You've heard of evidence, haven't you?"

Sam looked over at the detective and wanted to wipe the smug look off his face with a right cross, but he held his emotions in check. Will Powers was arrogant, brash, condescending and rude. But he wasn't stupid. He just needed more information before he acted on his request.

"You're not holding anything back are you Sam? Because that would not be a very nice thing now would it? After all, we are partners, and partners share and work together as a team."

Sam met his gaze and steeled his feelings against Will's brashness. No, Will was not stupid, but he played everything by the book and had little or no creativity and instinct. No, the problem with Will Powers was he'd lost his passion, either through his years at a desk sucking down cherry pie and drowning it in whole milk or by his lack of an outside life. He was so steeped in paperwork and standard operating procedure that he no longer had a handle on how the real world operated. Because of that, Will Powers would never play a hunch or take a risk, and that's what kept him average. But Will was right about one thing: Sam was keeping information from his partner. He just didn't trust him.

"If you want the truth, Will, I think we should be cooperating and working more closely with the FBI. They have resources that we don't. I've been talking to them."

Will Powers nearly launched his body across the desk at Sam so quickly that he moved back an inch or two in surprise.

"You what!"

"You heard me right. I spoke with their profiler, and he gave me some pretty good stuff. He's already started a file on it because they expect it to spread to other states and don't think we can handle it."

The frown on Will's face deepened.

"I didn't authorize you talking to him."

Sam ignored the comment.

"He says we're looking for someone who has little or no ties to the community or to family. Someone who flies under the radar so to speak. He says he's probably the most plain and boring fella you'd ever meet, has a mundane, unimportant job, has a religious background and some pretty twisted ideas about sex. He's an introvert and probably has trouble talking in a normal one-on-one conversation."

Will Powers reached into his desk drawer and pulled out another cherry pie.

"Those things are going to kill you, Will. You should cut back on them."

Will raised his right, middle finger up in front of his face in defiance.

"No one lives forever, Colton. Except maybe you."

Sam pursed his lips together tightly.

"Listen, Will, this guy wants to be caught. He's conflicted. That's why he leaves prints and DNA at the crime scenes. The FBI says a part of this guy knows he's doing wrong and he wants to be punished. The profiler says to look for commonalities."

Will unwrapped the red and white waxed paper from the pie and shoved a huge bite into his mouth. He chewed a moment and then swallowed too soon, almost choking himself. Sam Colton couldn't help but be reminded of Jabba the Hut.

"The victims all have something in common, Will."

Will Powers looked up and smiled condescendingly.

"Oh really? And what is that?"

Sam thought for a moment. *Maybe I'm wrong, maybe Will really is dumber than he looks.* But he let the thought slip away and answered the question.

"All of the victims were either prostitutes, having affairs, were homosexuals, or were registered sex offenders."

Will Powers looked over at him blankly.

"So? What's your point? Doesn't everybody have sex now days? Sexual immorality isn't a big deal anymore. People don't care about it like they used to."

Sam nodded.

"That's true, but this guy cares, and he cares enough to kill anyone who lives outside God's laws on sexual morality."

Will took another bite of his pie and chewed slowly. The *Star Wars* theme song flashed into Sam's head and he couldn't get rid of it. Jabba the Hut was all he could think.

"But where's the evidence, Sam? I don't see any proof. This is all just conjecture and speculation. I need something solid!"

Sam tried a different tact. He leaned forward in his chair, almost even with the front of Will's desk.

"I'm not asking you to arrest anyone, Will. I just want you to put someone under surveillance. There's a guy I've been watching, checking into his background. He works with Natalie and he seems to fit the profile from the FBI, at least so far. I still have more checking to do."

Will leaned back in his chair and it groaned under his weight. With some great effort he moved his feet up to the desk and plopped them onto a stack of paperwork.

"There's just one problem with your theory, Sam." Will smiled, all the while feeling superior. "The latest victim wasn't sexually immoral, not even close. He was a priest. So that blows your whole commonality-with-victims theory clean out of the water."

Sam Colton thought about it for a moment and then came to a crucial decision. He moved his hands to his lap while at the same time crossing his right ankle over his left thigh.

"Well, not really, Will. You see, you were right about one thing. I've been keeping something from you."

Will's face began to turn red, threatening his Jabba-sized head to explode from an embolism.

"The priest was having an affair with Natalie Katrell."

Will's feet dropped down off the desk and thudded onto the tile floor.

"What! Are you sure?"

Sam nodded up and down.

"Yes, I saw it myself and Natalie confirmed it."

Sam could sense a whiff of burning brain cells as Will Powers processed this new information. He waited for Will to state the obvious and wasn't disappointed.

"But that's wrong. He can't do that!"

Inside, Sam smiled, but his face remained stoic.

"Yes, that's the way I saw it too." And then Sam played dumb, something he wasn't very good at. "What do you think we should do, Will?"

Will thought for a moment more.

"We need to put Natalie Katrell under surveillance. But it shouldn't be you. You're too close to her and she might see you."

Then he made eye contact with Sam.

"Besides, I think you might be too emotionally involved with her and not thinking clearly."

Sam nodded.

"I don't disagree with you. What should I be doing?"

Will thought for a moment and Sam lingered impatiently as Will Powers pondered the obvious. Finally, his lips parted like the Red Sea and he delivered his proclamation.

"I want you to find out everything you can about this co-worker fella. What's his name?"

"His name is Mark. Mark Kayne."

Chapter Twenty-Nine

Natalie had slipped in through the back door of the church, and now she was alone in Tony Beddig's room, searching through his desk drawer. She didn't even know what she was looking for, just that she had to find it, that she needed closure for her own peace of mind.

She heard a sound off in another part of the church and her hands stopped moving. The sound stopped as quickly as it had started. She let out her breath and continued rummaging quietly through the pencil drawer. Disappointed, she found nothing and walked over to the book shelf.

She saw works by Henry Nouen, Madeleine L'Engle, C.S. Lewis and a bunch of other names she couldn't pronounce. Many of the books looked old and tired, their pages yellowed and folded and torn. She could relate.

Natalie picked up his Bible, an old King James with lots of writing in the margins. She opened it up and a paper fell out onto the floor. It was a photo. She bent down and scooped it up. Written on the back it said "Natalie Katrell and Amethyst-my chosen ones". She turned it over and gasped out loud. It was her and Amethyst in the park from two summer's ago.

She had come here for answers and gotten only more questions. How had he gotten it? Why? Was the entire town stalking her? Natalie opened her purse and put the picture inside the zipper pocket. Out of habit, she checked for the reassuring bulk of her 38 revolver.

She walked back over to the desk and opened up the laptop computer. The power cord was plugged in and the screensaver quickly came to life. Natalie moved the mouse and the words "Enter Password" popped into the middle of the screen. Natalie thought for a moment. *Did she dare to try?*

After a moment's hesitation, she quickly justified her intrusion. After all, he was dead and probably wouldn't care. Besides, she had an extreme need to know. She typed.

"Natalie"
The response came back quickly.

"Incorrect password. Access denied."
Disappointed, she typed again.

"stalker"
"Incorrect password. Access denied."
"MyChosenOnes"
"Incorrect password. Access denied."
"ILoveNatalie"
"Incorrect password. Access denied."
"StalkingNatalie"
"Incorrect password. Access denied."

For 15 minutes Natalie continued to type in anything she could think of but with negative results. Finally, she slammed the laptop closed in anger and lay her head on her arms atop the computer. She didn't hear the man walk up behind her.

He placed his hand on her neck and squeezed. Natalie's heart froze in her throat as the adrenaline flooded her blood stream.

Chapter Thirty

Hank Holden sat in his car outside Mark Kayne's apartment doing what he did best, eating Twinkies, drinking Mountain Dew and smoking Camel unfiltereds. The Mountain Dew gave him energy, the Twinkies satisfied his sweet tooth, and the Camels calmed his nerves and helped keep his weight down. It was a dietary system he'd been using for decades and it had never failed him. Yeah, sure, he was going to die someday because of it, but so what? Everyone had to die. At least this way he got to pick his poisons: either heart attack, stroke or cancer. He preferred a massive heart attack, no prolonged pain, no suffering. Quick and easy; that's how he wanted to go out.

He put his cigarette out in the ashtray and turned the page of the magazine he was reading: *"Bullets and Babes"*. He rotated the magazine sideways to get the full effect of the beautiful, bikini-clad brunette proudly displaying an ultra-light AR15 with a thirty-round magazine. Hank thought to himself *"Nice gun."*

His wife thought his choice in magazines was disgusting, and she was usually right, but that never stopped him from reading the articles and occasionally glancing at the pictures.

Hank took a second look and whistled out loud.

"Wow! That is a really nice firearm!" He looked around the car as a reflex action, but, of course, he was alone. "I'll have to get me one of those."

Hank had parked under a shade tree across from Mark Kayne's apartment to keep the car cool and to better hide his movement. He'd been there for four hours already and had seen nothing, but that didn't bother him so much. He was used to seeing nothing. Most of the time that's what happened on this job. He watched, ate Twinkies, drank Mountain Dew, smoked Camels and saw nothing at all. But he got paid whether he saw anything or not. It was kind of like a government job in that respect. Results are optional.

But he wasn't getting paid today. This was a favor for his long-time friend and ex-partner, Sam Colton. Hank saw movement in the upstairs window and lifted the binoculars to his eyes. It was just the wind blowing the curtain. He watched it flutter in the breeze for a moment and then lowered the binoculars to light another Camel. He rolled the window down to take advantage of the newfound breeze. It was a hot, July day. Thank God for the shade and the breeze. He would give it another hour and then head back to the air-conditioned office to write the report.

Hank had served in-country with Sam for one tour, and that time had bonded them forever. The military and Vietnam had bonded a lot of men, but most of them never stayed in contact like Sam and Hank had. They had gone to school together, enlisted together, and then been business partners for several years after Sam had retired from the force. What was it Sam had told him? "This is boring, and I'm too old for boredom. I don't have the time."

In the hot, steamy jungles of the war, Sam had saved Hank's life on several occasions and he was beholding to him forever. Hank saw movement again and lifted the binoculars up to his eyes. The curtains were blowing again. And then it occurred to him: *I don't remember the window being open when I came here?*

No sooner had the thought entered his mind than he felt the steel blade touch his throat. The knife sliced quickly, severing his artery, and Hank Holden watched his own life pump out onto the steering wheel of his car.

Finally, the gurgling sound stopped and the Camel slipped lazily from between his fingers and onto the wet magazine. The smoke drifted up, was caught on the breeze and rushed out the window into eternity.

Chapter Thirty-One

Natalie's fingers wrapped around her revolver as she drew it from her purse. In one, sweeping motion she turned and stepped away from the man, freeing her neck from his grasp. She pointed the gun out in front of her in a perfect isosceles stance directly at the center of the man's chest.

"I'm just the janitor."

Natalie watched as the blood drained from the old man's face. He was short, half bald and his back was hunched over as he leaned heavily on the broom he carried.

Natalie lowered her pistol and placed it back in her purse.

"Sorry. You startled me."

The color gradually returned to the man's face and the hint of a smile touched the corners of his mouth.

"I never saw a lady cop before. You always this nervous?"

Natalie lowered her head and blushed.

"I'm not a cop. And I never used to be this nervous. Sorry about that. My life has been a bit tense lately."

The old man smiled completely now.

He wrapped both hands tightly around the broom handle and leaned forward as he spoke.

"Yeah, well, I guess I can relate to that. Things have been a mite tense around here the past few days as well."

The old man looked her square in the eyes.

"Are you Natalie?"

Natalie cocked her head to one side and gave the old man

a quizzical stare.

"Yes, but how did you know that? What's going on?"

The old man motioned for her to sit down in the desk chair as he moved over and sat on the edge of the bed. His face was old and wrinkled, but when he spoke his eyes looked bright and young as can be.

"Tony told me all about you. He's been in love with you for over a year now."

Natalie shook her head.

"I don't understand. Up until a little while ago we didn't even know each other."

"Well, it's true that you didn't know him, but Tony's been watching you ever since he saw you and Amethyst playing in the park together. He used to go there the same time as you just so he could watch. He said it gave him hope to see how much you loved her."

Natalie squirmed uncomfortably in the chair.

"Was he stalking me?"

The old man laughed softly.

"Oh, heck Natalie, I don't even know what that means. It sounds like something a cop or a lawyer would say but a real person would just say you're following me too much and I don't much like it!"

Under better circumstances, Natalie would have liked the old man instantly, but these were not better times, so she remained aloof.

"You didn't answer my question. Was he stalking me?"

The old man looked down at the floor and then back up again quickly. He let out a heavy sigh.

"No, I suppose not. At least not in the dangerous, criminal sense. He just saw you in the park and then kept coming back to see you again. He did that for a year, but never saw you anywhere else until the hospital. That was really quite coincidental, but Tony read more into it than that. He wondered if maybe God hadn't brought you into his life or something. I told him it was just a coincidence, but he wouldn't believe me. He was always looking for something deeper, something with more purpose. Guess that's why he became a priest and I'm just the janitor."

Natalie lowered her head so he wouldn't see the tears forming in her eyes.

"How do you know all this about him?"

The old man laughed softly and leaned in closer.

"There are two kinds of confession, young lady: the kind you tell the church, and the kind you tell a friend. Tony told me everything."

Natalie looked back up with tears in her eyes.

"Did he ... ?

The old man nodded slowly.

"Yes, Natalie ... he did."

Natalie broke down now and sobbed openly. The old man rose from the bed and offered his shoulder to her which she gladly accepted.

"It's okay, sweetheart. Yes, of course he loved you. He was talking about leaving the priesthood, and I believe he would have too, eventually, once he figured everything out in his heart and his mind. He was a good man."

After a while, Natalie took a McDonald's napkin from her purse and dabbed at her wet eyes. The old man moved back to the bed and sat down again.

"My name is Jerry, by the way."

Natalie smiled and shook the hand that he offered her.

"It's a pleasure to meet you, Jerry."

Jerry was silent for a moment, but then he made eye contact with her again.

"So, Natalie, did you find what you were looking for?"

She rummaged through her purse and eventually brought out the picture of her and Natalie in the park.

"Yes, I think so. Do you think he would mind if I kept this?"

Jerry's eyes began to moisten as well.

"I see why he fell in love with you."

He got up off the bed and lifted up the mattress, reached inside and brought out a black, leatherbound book. He handed it to her.

"I think he would want you to have this too. These are all the things he wanted to tell you but didn't have the guts or was waiting for the right time."

Natalie reached out eagerly and grasped the book in both hands. She raised it to her face and smelled the perfect leather. It smelled like her new Bible.

"Thank you. May I have his Bible too?"

Jerry nodded and Natalie stood up and moved over to the book shelf again. She picked up the worn book and cradled both books as if they were children to be nurtured and protected.

"Thank you, Jerry. I appreciate everything."

She moved in to get one, last hug and Jerry put his arm around her, giving her an affectionate squeeze. Natalie pulled away and walked quickly out of the room.

Jerry watched after her, all the while contemplating the things that he hadn't told her.

Chapter Thirty-Two

"Of course I don't mind talking to you, officer. Why don't you have a seat?"

Sam Colton moved a stack of hard-covered commentaries off the chair beside him. Professor Harold Balyo looked to be about 87 years old, so he immediately garnered respect.

"Just put those on the floor, and I'll take care of them later on. I think they've been setting there for 6 months already. Guess I'm not that tidy eh?"

Sam smiled and sat down before talking.

"So, professor, what can you tell me about Mr. Kayne?"

"That depends."

Sam had just taken his notepad out of his breast pocket and immediately looked up.

"That depends on what?"

"That depends on which Mr. Kayne you're talking about. There were two of them you know."

Sam leaned back in his chair.

"Excuse me?"

"Yes, there were two Kayne boys that went here at about the same time. They were brothers as I recall."

Sam began to write furiously.

"Tell me everything. Start with Mark if you don't mind."

The old professor nodded and leaned forward in his over-stuffed desk chair.

"Yeah, sure, no problem. Mark was an excellent student, always got straight A's, always did everything by the book, never got into any trouble. Strictly from a teacher's point of view he was perfect, but … "

Sam stopped writing and looked up.

"But what?"

Professor Balyo leaned back and scratched his chin.

"I don't know. There was just something about him that made me nervous. He hardly ever talked; didn't have any friends; I never saw him with a female or anyone else for that matter around campus. He was pretty much the text book loner. Come to think of it I never really saw him much with his brother either. But he was polite and respectful, seldom made eye contact though. I always thought there was something strange about him, especially after that discussion in class."

As if he needed more prompting, Sam motioned with his hand for him to continue. The professor looked up at the ceiling as if remembering it from years ago.

"As I recall it was during a class on *Exposition of Genesis*, and his brother was in the class with him."

"What is his brother's name?"

"Kayne."

Sam looked up from his pad.

"No, I mean his first name."

"Kayne."

"His first name was Kayne?"

Professor Balyo nodded.

"Yes, and that's what makes it so memorable, because we were studying the passage in Genesis chapter 4 where Cain slew Abel and Mark had just asked a question about verse 9."

Sam nodded.

"And what does verse 9 say?"

"It says, *And the LORD said unto CAIN, Where is Abel thy brother? And he said, I know not: Am I my brother's keeper?*"

Sam looked confused.

"Okay, so Mark Kayne's brother is named Kayne Kayne and they were both in the class listening to a lecture on the Bible where Cain killed Abel." He thought about it for a moment. "Okay, you have my attention now. What happened that was so memorable?"

"Well Mark asked this one really profound question. He said "*If a person has two personalities, one good and one bad, and the bad personality murders someone, will both personalities go to hell?*"

Sam looked up after he finished writing.

"So what did you tell him?"

The older man leaned forward, placed his elbows on the desk and his palms against the side of his face.

"Well, I told him that it wasn't a question of which personality was guilty, but, rather, a question of which soul was guilty. Because God doesn't send personalities to hell, only souls. The Bible makes that pretty clear. But the boy's question intrigued me nonetheless, because no one had ever asked that before."

Sam's mind was racing now and his pulse had quickened even though he was sitting down. He thought to himself. *This is a spider web.* And then he thought *Mark is the spider and Natalie is the fly.*

"What about his brother, Kayne? Tell me about him."

The professor laughed out loud.

"Oh, Kayne was a wonderful boy, one of the most popular people on campus, good at sports, good with the ladies, he was a real social hub if ever there was one."

Sam jotted down some more notes.

"What else can you tell me."

"Oh, he wasn't as good a student as Mark by a long shot. I always got the impression he was too busy to study and so he just did what he had to do to get by. He usually got B's and C's, at least in my classes. You can get both their transcripts at the office I'm sure."

Sam nodded again, all the while looking pensively at the notepad in front of him.

"So what did Kayne look like?"

The professor turned around in his chair and started searching through the book shelf beside him.

"Kayne and Mark didn't look anything alike despite the fact that they were twins. I have a picture right here in the yearbook if I can find the right year."

"What? They were twins but didn't look anything alike? That doesn't make any sense."

Harold Balyo laughed again. He pulled a hard-covered yearbook off the shelf and started leafing through it.

"Of course it does, my friend! They weren't identical twins; they were fraternal twins. You know, they were in the womb together but not created from the same egg. Kayne was a big fella, but Mark was slight."

The professor held the book open to a certain page and passed it over the desk to Sam.

"Right there where my finger is. They're right next to each other. See?"

Sam nodded.

"Yes, you're right. They don't even look related."

He ripped off a blank sheet from his notepad and used it to mark the page before closing it.

"Professor Balyo do you mind if I hold on to this for a

while? I'll get it back to you. I promise."

Sam stood up and reached his right hand over to the older man.

"Thanks you for your time, Doctor Balyo. I appreciate it. You've been very helpful."

The professor also stood shakily to his feet, using the desk top to help push himself up.

"Not a problem Officer. Just glad I could help."

The two men shook hands.

"So are you going to tell me what this is all about, Officer Colton?"

Sam knew better than to tell him the whole truth. After all, he didn't really know the whole truth himself.

"It's part of an ongoing criminal investigation, so I'm not at liberty to divulge that information."

The professor narrowed his eyes skeptically.

"Come on now, officer, this isn't a spring chicken you're talking to. Just tell me which one is in trouble. You owe me that much."

Sam smiled inside. He really liked this guy, and he had been very helpful.

"It's Mark that we're looking into."

"Really? That surprises me."

Sam hesitated at the doorway.

"And why is that?"

"Well, primarily because Kayne is the one who was sent to prison for raping Dean Kimble's wife. Mark graduated summa cum laude, but Kayne never made it past his junior year."

Sam Colton's jaw made a resounding thud as it hit the carpeted floor.

Chapter Thirty-Three

"*In the land of play,*
in the land of dreams,
it's always fun or so it seems."

Natalie sat on the largest of the granite headstones beside her dead boyfriend's grave as Amethyst jumped from one granite marker to the next, singing all the while as she played. She loved Amethyst and she loved taking care of her and being a mother, but ... sometimes ...

"Come and play with me, Mommy!"

Natalie looked up with tears in her eyes and answered as loudly as she could without letting her voice break.

"In a minute, honey. I just need a little more time to rest."

It had always been difficult, working long days, coming home exhausted both physically and emotionally, and then sometimes having to feign excitement over playing dress up and Barbies and watching movies that she'd never see on her own. It had always been the sum of her life, always been her lot, always taking care of others and never taken care of herself.

"I'm sorry, God. I know I'm feeling sorry for myself, and I know that I shouldn't and that you probably don't feel sorry for weak people like me."

Then she looked up at the sky as if she could actually see God himself.

"But I really am pitiful, aren't I?"

She squeezed the leather cover of Tony's diary as she

spoke.

"I mean look at me. I hooked up with a real jerk who left me. And yes, I know I'm not supposed to have sex until I get married, but that's water under the bridge so can we just drop it for now?"

"In the land of play,
in the land of dreams ..."

She glanced over at Amethyst hopping from one stone to the next and wondered if a good parent would stop her daughter from desecrating the dead. But she was too weary to care.

"Then I fell in love with a priest of all men, and that probably really made you mad because I guess technically he was already married to you." She paused, "But I gotta tell you that whole concept just sounds ridiculous to me. You shouldn't be married to another man; it's just not right. After all, it's hard enough for a girl to find a decent man without God almighty putting the best of the lot off the market. I mean give me a break, will ya?"

She ran the fingers of her left hand across the bumpy leather of the book on her lap. Still, she hadn't opened it up yet. She was terrified of what she might find inside its cover. Amethyst sang louder

"It's always fun or so it seems."

It had been fun, right up until whoever it was put a bullet in Tony's head. She glanced down at the book, then over to Amethyst, then to the freshly dug dirt of the grave, then back down to the book again. Slowly, she opened it up to a random page in the middle.

"I saw her in the park again today playing with her daughter. They are both so beautiful together. They paint a picture

of Christ' love for all mankind: sacrificial, giving, passion-
ate, and yet ... still ... they fit together and seem to complete
one another."

Natalie noted the date and looked over at her daughter. Yes, she was precious, and she did mean everything to her. She kept her going sometimes and always gave her a reason to live. Oddly enough, she had forgotten about that the past few weeks. She thought it ironic that she had been transfixed with Tony, had temporarily forgotten about her daughter, and now, after he was dead, his words from the grave were reminding her of the most important person in her life. She skipped to further in the back of the book.

"I know that I'm doing wrong, at least in the eyes of the
church, but I can't help myself. For the first time in my life I
feel alive like never before. Yes, I know that I've pledged my
whole life to you and there should be no room for another,
but ... I have to tell you the truth. There are things that you
can't give me. You made me a man with desires and needs
that are more than spiritual. You can't hug me or even touch
me, but ... Natalie ... she gives the best hugs."

A tear ran down Natalie's cheek and she quickly wiped it away with her left hand. She turned several pages further into the book and read more. It was in letter form.

"My dearest Natalie,

You have changed my life for the better. So many things I
would never have felt and known have come from you. I feel
like I understand humanity more after having met you and
held you and listened to your hopes and dreams and all you
hold dear. Yes, there is the guilt of my broken vow, but I can't
help that. God and I have talked about it at length, and ...

I have decided to leave the priesthood to spend my life with you. I haven't told the church yet, but I will soon. According to the rules of the church I will still be able to serve, but in a lesser capacity.

The tears poured freely down Natalie's face now and she didn't try to wipe them all away. Eventually, they dripped off her cheeks and onto the diary pages. It was dated the day of his death. All Natalie could think was *He loved me. He loved me. He really did love me.* And then she found herself speaking out loud. "I love you."

"I love you too, Mommy!"

Natalie looked up and reached out to Amethyst who quickly rushed into her open arms and climbed atop her lap.

"Why are you crying, Mommy?"

The diary had fallen to the grass, so she reached down with one hand and picked it up and set it beside her.

"Oh, honey, I was just reading a sad story that's all. Nothing to worry about."

Amethyst beamed.

"I got an idea! Let's make the story happy again, then you don't got to cry no more! Tell me a happy story, Mommy!"

Natalie looked her dear one straight in the eyes and smiled as she spoke softly.

"You are my story sweetheart, and you are the happiest story a Mommy could ever have."

Amethyst kissed Natalie on the cheek and slid down off her lap.

"Okay Mommy. Let's get a five-dollar pizza and watch *Barbie in the Land of Fairies*!"

Natalie laughed as they walked away.

"Oh my! That is a good one! What shall we put on our

five-dollar pizza?"

Amethyst didn't answer. She just skipped along in front of her mother as she sang:

> *"In the land of play,*
> *in the land of dreams,*
> *it's always fun or so it seems."*

Chapter Thirty-Four

Sam Colton recognized Kayne immediately from the photo in the prison file in front of him. During the 30 minutes he'd been waiting to see him, he had read through it carefully.

Kayne had been raised by his father Gerald Kayne in Bath, Michigan after his mother had been stabbed to death in her bedroom. Mark and Kayne had watched the brutal murder at the age of 4 years old. The killer had never been caught.

Kayne had a long history of trouble with the police, but the rape of the Dean's wife had been his first conviction. He'd spent 5 years in prison. He was only on the street for less than a month when he raped another woman and brutally beat her, permanently disfiguring her face. The case had been thrown out of court on a technicality and he was soon out on the street again. Within three months he was back in prison on an armed robbery charge. Kayne had already served four years of a seven-year sentence.

He was in orange coveralls and wore shackles on his wrists and ankles. According to his file, he fought frequently and was less than a model inmate in nearly every regard. Kayne plopped himself down heavily in the chair. Sam noticed how heavily muscled the man was and raised his awareness up a notch or two. The guard left them alone in the room, but Sam knew they were watching through the one-way window.

Sam made eye contact with him for the first time and his

blood turned to ice. This man was cold.

"Thanks for seeing me, Kayne."

The bearded inmate stared at him through ice-covered eyes, but said nothing in return.

"I'm here to talk about your brother, Mark."

Sam thought he saw a flicker of something resembling humanity in Kayne's eyes, but it was only there for a moment and then gone quicker than it had come.

"When was the last time you saw your brother?"

Kayne's face remained passive and unmoving. His voice remained silent.

"Can you tell me where he is right now?"

Kayne turned his face up toward the ceiling as if interested in the ceiling fan. There was no ceiling fan.

"Can you tell me about your brother's personality?"

To his surprise, Kayne laughed out loud. Sam cocked his head to one side.

"Did I say something funny?"

Kayne stopped laughing and turned toward him, glaring with those ice eyes again.

"You don't know ... do you?"

Sam hated playing cat and mouse, especially when he was the mouse. Under the circumstances, he did his best to sound less than stupid. He decided to be open and honest.

"We know very little about him. He seems to keep to himself, never been in trouble, doesn't date, has no friends to speak of. It's almost as if he doesn't exist except on paper."

Kayne crossed his arms on his massive chest as best he could with the shackles hindering him.

"Why do you want to know about him?"

Sam leaned forward a bit and turned on the small recorder.

"I'm working on a serial killing, and your brother fits the profile. I'm just doing background research right now, looking for things that might make sense."

Kayne's eyes perked up.

"The Vanilla Killer?"

Sam's pulse quickened, but he worked hard to keep his poker face. *How did he know that name?*

"Yes, that's the one. The case has us a bit baffled and we're checking into anything that might lead somewhere."

"Forget about it!"

"Excuse me?"

"You'll never catch him. He's smarter than you."

Sam forced himself to laugh.

"Yeah, well, most people can say that, but, unfortunately, I'm the man on the case. So what can you tell me that helps?"

Kayne turned away and looked at the wall.

"So why the hell should I help you?"

At first Sam had no idea what to say. Truth be known, Kayne was right. The killer was smarter than him. In fact, Sam had a feeling that Kayne was smarter than him as well. But Sam had one thing in his favor: he had nothing to lose. In a moment of blind inspiration he blurted out.

"Because Mark is on the outside and you're stuck in here."

The large man gritted his teeth and Sam could hear his molars grinding together.

"I hate that little freak!"

"Is he a killer?"

Kayne laughed without hesitation.

"Yes ... and ... No. In a manner of speaking of course."

Sam forced a soft smile across his frustrated lips.

"Can you be a little less cryptic for me, especially seeing as though I'm not all that smart."

Kayne moved his stubbled face closer and whispered in a hoarse, guttural spewing.

"My brother is crazy!"

Sam cocked his head to one side.

"I didn't expect you to say that. What exactly do you mean by crazy?"

"I mean he's a damn lunatic! He even scares me sometimes. Half the time I don't know who I'm talking to. It's like he has different people inside him that come out to play sometimes and some of them are really nasty."

"Do you mean he has a split personality?"

Kayne grunted and looked down.

"I don't know anything about that psycho mumbo jumbo. I don't even believe in all that crap. I just know that he's evil deep down inside and he pretends to be good. That bugs me more than anything. He's not being honest about it. Yeah, sure, you look at me and see a guy who hurts people and steals and all that shit. But deep down inside I know who I am and why I got this way. I'm honest about my evil and I gotta think that carries some weight with the Lord. You think so too, don't you?"

Sam didn't answer. Sometimes he wondered where the line was between crazy and evil, assuming there was a line separating them.

"I mean, hell, look at me. I'm here in chains, suffering for my convictions. I hurt people and I like it. They make me mad so I have to do it. That's just the way it is. They should just shut up when I tell them to and they won't get hurt. It's their own damned fault. It's cause and effect ya know? They won't shut up so I gotta beat the crap out of 'em. They got it coming. But that's not my point, ya see? My point is that I'm up front about it. I says to the guy, either shut up or I'll kick yer ass! That way I stay an honest man and I can live with myself after I hurt 'em. You understand?"

Sam nodded.

"Yeah, sure, I can respect that. So what is the difference with your brother then? What makes him less honest than you?"

Kayne grit his teeth and ground them together in an attempt to hold his temper.

"I already told you that! Don't make me repeat myself! I don't have time for this bull! I can't be sitting around here all day jaw jacking with some stupid cop. I got important stuff to do!"

Sam got the impression that he was supposed to ask Kayne about his own life, but he resisted the snare.

"So, if I got this straight then, you are honest about your crimes and Mark is deceitful because he pretends to be a good person even when he's doing bad things?"

Kayne nodded angrily.

"Yeah, see you got it. Now stop playing stupid cuz I don't want to repeat myself again."

Sam nodded blankly.

"Sure. I got it. So what kind of bad things does he do?"

Kayne looked up and smiled.

"That's for me to know and you to find out!"

Sam moved uncomfortably in his chair. Some days he hated the criminal justice system. If he had his druthers, he'd just as soon tie Kayne to his chair and torture the information out of him. It would be faster and save the tax payer's money.

"I'm not asking you to rat him out. I just want you to tell me if he's capable of taking another human life."

Kayne sneered back at him.

"You know damn well he can do it. I can see that much in your own eyes. You done it yourself. I can see it in your eyes from here."

Sam's eyes narrowed and he pursed his lips tighter. He didn't like being read by a con. They were not book learned, but so many of them possessed the uncanny ability to read a man's heart.

"That's right. I've killed before. Many times. But I never enjoyed it. I don't like doing it and I only do it to protect the innocent. You know the question I'm asking. I know you do, so stop playing me like a fiddle. I don't like it!"

Kayne smiled and leaned closer until his elbows touched the table top.

"Now see. That wasn't so hard now was it? I just want a little honesty that's all. You're a killer. I'm a killer. Mark's a killer. It don't matter the details. But since you been honest with me, I'll talk a little more."

Sam waited. Kayne looked up and appeared to be chewing on his tongue as he listened to some unheard voice.

"You wanna know if baby brother kills for fun, and the truth is, not only yeah, but hell yeah!"

Sam didn't move. He wasn't even breathing.

"But that's not how you can catch him. In order to stop him, you have to find the teacher."

Kayne hesitated, knowing that he was making Sam wait and squirm.

"You gotta find ... *Daddy dearest*!"

Before Sam could speak, Kayne moved to his feet and yelled for the guard. They came in and took him away, leaving Sam alone to think about all he'd heard.

Chapter Thirty-Five

The little boy squirmed uncomfortably on a foam-covered diaper-changing table, and his feet stuck off the end of it clenched together, barely able to handle the pain.

"Hold still, boy! I'm almost done!"

The man shoved the needle into the side of the boy's head as far as it would go and wiggled the metal shaft back and forth.

Mark screamed in agony as Kayne held down his brother's head.

"Shut up or it will hurt worse. You're going to ruin it if you don't hold still and then I'll have to do it all over again. The evil must be purged!"

Mark opened his eyes and saw his brother's terrified face looking down on him. His five-year-old brain often wondered *Why me? Why never Kayne? What's wrong with me?*

"Almost done and then you can watch cartoons."

He felt a stabbing and then a twist inside his brain until something snapped.

"Ahhh! Stop it Daddy! Please stop it!"

Mark woke up in bed drenched with sweat and a throbbing in his brain. He reached up and grabbed his head in both hands and squeezed as hard as he could. The pills didn't work anymore and the dreams kept coming back more and more and more.

He rolled over onto his side and curled into the fetal position. He didn't want to do it. He loved her. But he knew the throbbing would continue until the sin was purged, and it was becoming unbearable. She should have been good. She should have remained blameless. It was her fault. The world is cause and effect. She sinned, therefore, the sin must be cleansed.

And there can be no remission of sins without the shedding of blood. He spoke out loud.

"I'm sorry, Natalie. I love you."

He looked up to the life-sized picture of her on the ceiling above his bed and tears ran down both his cheeks.

"I love you and I have to save you."

§ § §

Sam Colton stood over his friend's freshly buried grave. They had been through a war together; they had watched each other's kids; their wives had gone shopping together every week for decades.

Now, Hank Holden was dead.

Sam clenched the sand in his left hand and squeezed it as hard as he could, either unwilling or unable to let it go. He knew the killer. He knew his address. He knew how to stop him. All he had to do was ...

"I've never broken the law before, Hank. But I know how to do it. It would be easy. It would be deserved. It would be a righteous killing that saves many lives. I would never be caught and Natalie and Amethyst would live."

He clenched his teeth together as he remembered the day before with Kayne at the prison. The man was crazy and so was his brother. They were both killers, demons against society that needed to be exorcized. He wanted to and a part of him said it was right. But another part ...

"If I kill him. Is it really wrong? I was trained for it. No one else can do it like me. I was made for this. And even if I do get caught and go to prison, well, my life is almost gone. It could be the last service to society I ever perform. It's a good thing. Isn't it? Would God really care if one, sick son of a bitch dies?"

There was no answer from the grave. Hank Holden lay cold and silent. Sam threw the fistful of sand onto the ground with one, viscous cast. He spit onto the grass as he walked away.

"Damn it, Hank! You were never much use when you were alive either!"

Sam Colton stalked out of the cemetery to plot his next move.

Chapter Thirty-Six

Dear Diary,

I regret to announce that Kayne has decided to purge the evil. I did my best to dissuade him, but he was determined. But I haven't given up yet. Unbeknownst to him I have a plan. Already I've put it in place. It is almost fool proof.

I hate the sin too. I always have, but ... I think it is true that we can become that which we hate most, if we allow it. We all are accountable under the Lord. And that means that indeed, yes, I truly am my brother's keeper.

Mark stopped writing and looked over at Natalie. She was working hard and totally oblivious to his gaze. But Mark knew the truth. She probably wasn't even working. She was probably sending private emails, which, of course, is against company policy. She shouldn't do that. Mark never sent personal emails.

And then the most bizarre thought popped into his head, and he had no idea where it came from. *No, Mark. You never write personal emails on company time, but you write in your diary. What can be more personal than that?*

Mark looked around as if expecting to see someone standing there, but there was no one else in his cubicle. *There are none righteous. No! Not one!* There it was again! He looked around. Then stood up and peered over the top of his orange cubicle wall. He gazed around three hundred and sixty degrees, but no one was there. All his co-workers were silently working at their desks. He shook his head and sat back down in his chair. He picked up his pen and wrote in perfect penmanship.

I think someone is watching me. Perhaps I should get back to my work.

Mark closed the green, spiral notebook and placed it safely inside his pencil drawer along with the pen. He looked over at Natalie. She was beautiful to behold. He looked back at his computer screen and typed:

Using the special wrench provided in the installation kit, turn Nut (A) on bolt (F) being careful not to overtorque the nut.

Caution: It is especially important that you not cause too much stress on the nut as it may cause the unit to malfunction and be rendered unusable.

§ § §

Natalie had always been exceptionally clever when she goofed off at work. Even now, to the casual passer-by, they would believe that she was typing furiously on her Rasco Model 2300 Industrial Kitchen Blender manual. After all, that's what was showing on the screen in front of her. But way off in the lower-left-hand corner of the screen was another window that was only partially visible. It contained an email she was writing to Sam Colton, whom she hadn't spoken to in several days.

Dear Sam,
I'm sorry I haven't spoken to you in so long. I've had a rough week. I'm also sorry to hear that your friend died. I read about it in the paper. Okay, enough with the pleasantries.

I have to tell you that I'm a bit scared and was hoping that we could start shooting together again. When I came back to work here they searched me and ordered me not to bring my gun on company property. I went along with them, but still have my pistol concealed in that belly band holster you told me about. (It makes me look five pounds heavier and I don't like that, but it's better than going unprotected.)

Where have you been and what have you been up to? I don't mean to grill you but you were always very present and now you are mysteriously absent. I'm sorry if I yelled at you too much. Truth is I fell in love with a priest and knew it was wrong, but then everytime I saw you it reminded me I was doing something wrong. Did I mention I have a temper? It's just that I was so happy for the first time in years and I didn't want it to end. I'm wondering if maybe God is judging me and Tony's death is partly my fault for causing him to sin. Can we talk about that?

Also, I spoke with the janitor at the church and he's a really nice man named Jerry. He told me that Tony loved me and was thinking about leaving the priesthood to marry me. He gave me Tony's Bible and his diary which I've read three times. He really did love me.

Okay, I'm not going to ramble on like we're both a couple of school girls here, but truth is I don't have any female friends so I'm forced to treat you like you're one of the girls. Sorry about that.

Okay, like I said, I'm scared. Someone has been coming into my apartment while I'm gone. I've been putting that tape on the door like you showed me and it's been broken three times now. Last night someone came in while we were sleep-

ing and I just can't have that. Nothing was disturbed, and Amethyst was okay, but I just get this image of some creep standing over my bed watching me while I sleep. Can you please call me before bed time tonight, because I really don't think I can sleep until I know the apartment is secure?

Sorry to be such a pest and a burden. I don't mean to play the helpless female card, but I guess I need more help than I care to admit.

All the best.

Natalie

No sooner had she pressed the "return" key than her boss spoke to her from behind.

"Natalie! What are you doing?"

Her heart jumped up into her throat and she had to hold both hands together in her lap to keep them from trembling. When she talked, she tried to sound casual.

"Oh, hi Dave. You startled me."

He looked down at her and tilted his head to one side just a little bit.

"Why? Is there something you have to hide?"

Natalie laughed innocently.

"No, of course not, Dave. I'm just working hard on the Rasco Model 2300 Industrial Kitchen Blender manual and I was so engrossed in it that I didn't see you walk up."

Dave's eyes narrowed a bit before he spoke.

"Hmmm, yes, I see. That's an important manual. Will it be out by tomorrow?"

Sensing what was coming next, Natalie's smile started to fade.

"Ahh, well, no, not quite. I can have it shipped day after

tomorrow though."

But Dave's head was already wagging back and forth like a short-haired Doberman.

"Well, no that's just not going to cut it, Natalie. I promised that one to Rasco by tomorrow. You know that. Better stay late tonight until it's finished."

He started to walk away but then stopped and looked back. He glanced down at her screen as if searching for something. Natalie swivelled around in her chair and looked into his face.

"Is that all, Dave?"

He turned and met her gaze.

"Yes, of course. I just want to be clear that I need that manual in my inbox by tomorrow morning when I come in. Is that clear?"

She nodded. "Yes, Dave. It's crystal clear."

After he walked away, Natalie slumped down into her chair and fumed silently. Then she picked up the phone to call the babysitter.

The man across the aisle looked over at her and smiled. Natalie saw his look and it sent a tremble down her spine.

Chapter Thirty-Seven

S am Colton felt his pants vibrating and nearly fell off his chair. Quickly, he stood up from his desk and took the Blackberry out of his pocket. He held it out in front of him like it was a rattlesnake. It vibrated again and he nearly dropped it. He walked over to the admin cubicle and handed it to Peggy Mathers.

"What's wrong now, Sam?"

"I don't know. It keeps vibrating! Why won't it ring like a regular phone?"

Peggy laughed and took the Blackberry from his outstretched palm.

"It says you have an email."

Sam looked puzzled.

"Really? That thing has email too?"

Peggy gave him an impatient look and then wagged a rebuking finger his way.

"Sam, are you telling me that you still haven't taken the online tutorial for your Blackberry yet?"

"I don't have time for that. I'm trying to catch bad guys. I don't even like computers!"

"Well, Sam, if you're going to maximize your natural bad-guy catching skills, then it's important that you know how to use all the tools in your toolbox. You can do a Google search with this thing, listen to the radio, watch TV, check your email. You can even send a tweet and check your facebook."

Sam Colton clenched his jaw firmly.

"I don't have a facebook, and the last time I saw a tweet I ran over it with my truck! So can you please pretend I'm seventy years old and show me how to read my email message?"

Peggy shook her head from side to side disapprovingly.

"Okay, Sam, but this is the last time I help you. I want you to read that manual."

"Yeah, sure, Peggy. You know I will."

She raised an eyebrow at him as she pushed buttons on the tiny box. She read the subject line and smiled.

"Oh, Sam. It's from a woman and she misses you. She wants you to come over to her apartment tonight!"

He reached over quickly and grabbed the Blackberry from her hands.

"Give me that thing, Peggy! Can't you respect my privacy?"

"Hey, you told me to read it! You are such a sly dog! What is she like?"

Sam looked at the little screen and read Natalie's name but then it went dark.

"Hey, it went blank on me!"

Peggy laughed.

"Push the mouse button, silly!"

Sam shook his head and stormed back into his office. Once he was sitting down, he rummaged through his left-hand drawer until he found the User's Manual. He quickly scanned the section titled "Getting Started" and then pressed the correct button. The screen lit up and he read through Natalie's email message. When he put the dataphone back into his pocket he was clearly disconcerted.

"Jerry the janitor gave her a diary and a Bible?"

His face turned to scowl toward the wall.

"That's evidence in a murder case. It might be important!"

He picked up the rotary dial desk phone and dialed in Natalie's work number. It rang but immediately switched to voice mail. He thought to himself *Infernal machines! They're taking over the world!*

Sam grabbed his notebook and headed toward the door. Then he paused, wondering, *Should I invite Detective Cherry Pie Powers?* He shook his head and continued out to his car. Sam Colton worked alone.

§ § §

"What do you mean I can't speak to your janitor? Is it Catholic classified? Is he dead now too? What's going on here? I've got a lead and I need to talk to your custodian right now!"

Father Bevere looked at him and smiled.

"Detective Colton, please stop yelling at me long enough to read my reverent lips. For the last time! We don't have a paid custodian! We're a small parish and we just can't afford it, especially in this economy."

For the first time since walking into the church office, Sam appeared to grasp what Father Bevere was saying.

"Do you mean to tell me that you don't have a janitor named Jerry who works here?"

The father nodded up and down. Sam looked toward the crucifix hanging on the wall beside him.

"So who the hell cleans the church?"

Sam winced at his own thoughtless spontaneity and then reworded his question.

"Oh, sorry, father. What I meant to say was *So who cleans*

this lovely cathedral?"

Father Bevere smiled as he answered.

"We have an elderly couple, Rose and Jeb Waite who come in to clean every week. They've been doing it for twenty years now. God bless their souls."

And then Father Bevere looked at him sternly for the first time.

"So, tell me Detective Colton, when was the last time you went to confession?"

Sam jumped up from the chair and quickly excused himself.

"Thanks, Father Bevere, but I really have to be going now. Something came up that I really have to check on. Thanks so much. "

Father Bevere watched as Sam Colton rushed up and out of the room. He heard the outside door slam shut before his heart went back to grieving for his friend, Father Tony Beddig.

Chapter Thirty-Eight

"**M**om I have to work very late tonight to get this manual out, maybe even past midnight."

Natalie nodded her head up and down into the phone.

"So can you go over to the sitter's house and pick up Amethyst for me? It would be better if she spent the night with you. Then I can come there straight from work and just sleep on your couch tonight."

She nodded again and then smiled.

"Thanks Mom. You're wonderful! Oh, and one other thing. Maybe you could stop by my apartment and pick up a few Barbie movies before getting her. She would really love that. You still have the key don't you?"

Natalie smiled again and then hung up the phone before turning back to work furiously on the Rasco Industrial Kitchen Blender. All the while she thought to herself. *I'm happy to have my job, especially in this economic downturn. I love my job! I love my job! I love Rasco blenders! Rasco rocks!*

She got that feeling like someone was watching her but didn't look up. She already knew it was Mark from across the aisle. She had never seen him this brazen and bold before. And to think that she'd almost taken him out to lunch. But she ignored the feeling of being watched and focused back on her blender manual. Besides, it didn't matter. There were security cameras everywhere in the building, along with security officers and lots of co-workers. She was probably safer here than at home.

§ § §

Across the aisle, Mark pulled out his spiral notebook and continued to write.

Kayne is doing it tonight. He told me so. I don't know all the details, but I just know that I have to stop him. Natalie is my friend. Someday she's going to fall in love with me and marry me. I know it.

He stopped writing and looked over at her desk. She was gone. Quickly, he looked around and saw her coming back down the aisle with a fresh cup of coffee. He breathed a sigh of relief.

I can't let her out of my sight tonight, not even for a moment. It's too dangerous for her. This is my last chance to do something good and noble and righteous.

He put his pen back down and returned the notebook to the drawer. Suddenly, an email message popped up onto his screen. It was from Natalie. All it said was: *Please stop staring at me. I don't like it!*

Mark's eyes misted over as he read. He typed a few keystrokes to delete the message, but something wouldn't let him press the "Enter" key. He read the message again and again and again. He never deleted it. Instead, a smile gradually came over his face and he wiped the tears from his eyes. He looked over at Natalie, daring her to confront him. She glanced over, saw his gaze and then turned back to her computer. He heard her disapproving sigh and it stung him to the core. *She doesn't love me.* Someone had once written that anger is a secondary emotion. At that moment, Mark knew it to be true, as his pain slowly turned to anger.

§ § §

Later in the day, Natalie glanced back over at Mark's cubicle, and she saw that he was gone. She looked at the clock on her computer. Only 4:10. He had never left early before. His briefcase and umbrella were gone as well. He never left them in his office. Natalie turned and looked down the aisle both ways and verified that he was nowhere to be seen before breathing a sigh of relief. It didn't matter. She was safe here, and she had to get this manual done before she could see her daughter. That's all she cared about - Amethyst - her flesh and blood, her little one who loved Barbie and her mother, who needed her for love and protection and everything else. Amethyst was her sole reason for living, so she refocused and typed as fast as she could.

For the first time, she finally realized that, perhaps, *she* needed Amethyst as much as Amethyst needed her. With a few well-placed keystrokes, Natalie pulled up an email window and typed out a short message to Sam Colton.

Sam,

Have to work very late tonight. Amethyst is at my Mom's. All is well. I'll stay there tonight. Keep your powder dry.

Natalie

Natalie smiled at the cleverness of her last sentence. She knew he would get a kick out of that last line. They could meet up tomorrow and she was sure he would help secure her apartment. After all, he was the hero type, a real cowboy, the last John Wayne. And then she thought, *No, he's a sheep dog, just like me.*

Natalie pressed "Enter" and quickly went back to typing about the evil tormentor "Rasco the Industrial Blender". With any luck, she could be out of here by midnight.

§ § §

Anna Katrell was 55 years old but didn't really think of herself as old. After all, her personal motto was, *it's not the years; it's the miles.* Then again, if she was truly honest with herself, then she had to admit that she had more miles on her than a Model T Ford, and the undercarriage as well as the engine was getting a bit rickety. And Anna's miles were rough, not smooth, easy highway miles, but tough, city miles and back roads with lots of bumps and potholes. Despite all that, her attitude remained pretty good. She didn't allow herself to hate men openly, although the temptation sometimes got the best of her when she was with her daughter, Natalie.

"Hey Gramma! We gotta hurry so are pizza don't get cold afore the movie!"

Anna moved doggedly up the stairs to her daughter's apartment, all the while saying to herself, *"It's not the years, it's the miles. Have these steps always been this steep?"*

I'll be right there, honey. Just wait up for Gramma." When she reached the top she was breathing hard.

"Open the door, Gramma! I gotta get the Barbie movies!"

Anna fumbled with her purse for the keys, then finally managed to get the key in the lock and turn it. She opened the door and Amethyst rushed on in to her bedroom. Anna followed and shut the door behind her.

"Hurry, sweetheart! It's almost 5 o'clock and we don't have much ... " But her words were cut short as a strong arm wrapped around her neck from behind and then pushed her face against the door. She struggled and opened her mouth to scream, but as soon as she did, a smelly rag was placed over her nose and mouth. Anna smelled the toxic fumes and almost at once became dizzy. Her last thoughts were of Amethyst and what would become of her.

The old woman slumped to the floor just as Amethyst ran back into the room.

"Gramma, I got the ... " Amethyst stopped and opened her eyes wide in horror at the man standing over her Grandmother. He smiled at her, showing a full set of old and yellow teeth.

"Why hello, there Amethyst. Your Gramma has fallen down. Will you help me pick her up?"

Amethsyt hesitated but then took a step forward.

"Is she okay?"

The man nodded his head.

"Yes, but we need to hurry and get her to the doctor. Please help me."

Amethyst moved forward and knelt down beside her Gramma. The smelly rag closed over her nose and she was out in seconds. The Barbie videos slipped from her limp hands and hit the floor with a thud. The man stood up and smiled.

"Oh my. That was easy."

He took out the roll of duct tape in his pack and got right to work.

Chapter Thirty-Nine

I t was just past 9PM and Detective Will Powers sat outside Natalie Katrell's apartment. He'd been there for two hours already, just watching. He had been here several times the past few days, but nothing had turned up. He was starting to believe that Sam Colton was blowing smoke up his ... Hey, wait! A man was walking up to the door. Will raised the binoculars up to his eyes and scanned for a closer look. The man was overdressed for a hot and muggy summer night with a jacket, long pants and a hat pulled down over his eyes. Will picked up his digital camera, zoomed in and snapped a few closeups.

On the seat beside him was a folder. He picked it up and sorted through the papers until he found the photo Sam Colton had given him. He held it up to the neon light of the lamp post and thought to himself, *It could be him. It's hard to tell though with the hat pulled down over his eyes.*

The man at the door hesitated, looked around and then inserted a key in the door. He had a little trouble and wiggled it back and forth before it turned. Will smiled. *It's a copy of the original and doesn't work as well. This could be our bad guy.*

Will started to get out of the car and stopped. He looked down at his cell phone on the seat and frowned. He should call Sam. But he hated Sam. Then Will smiled. *I'll send him a text message. He won't even be able to read it and I'll be covered.* As quickly as his clumsy oversized fingers would move, he typed out the following message:

Sam, At Katrell's apt. Suspect entering. Going in. Need backup! Have probable cause. Powers

When Will's overweight body stepped out of the car, the frame lifted up several inches. He was wearing a short-sleeved, white dress shirt, bountifully stained with armpit sweat. He paused long enough to sniff his left arm and shrugged before pulling on his suit jacket. Nothing he could do about the smell. They paid him to catch bad guys, not to look and smell good. Will reached the apartment complex door and pulled on the handle but it was locked. He reached over with his right hand and started randomly pressing buzzer buttons until someone answered. Finally, a voice came back.

"Yes, who is this?"

Will grinned from ear to ear. He liked this part.

"This is Police Detective Will Powers. Buzz me in!"

A few seconds passed, the buzzer sounded and Will pulled the door open. *Easy. Easy as pie!*

§ § §

Inside Natalie's apartment, the hooded man released the button allowing Will Powers access. He reached over and unlocked the door, then he walked into the bedroom. As he waited for Will to enter, he rummaged through Natalie's dresser. He found some particularly sexy lingerie, pink, his favorite color, and stuffed it in his jacket pocket. That was all he'd come for. He just wanted something to remember her by.

The apartment door creaked open slowly and the man smiled with satisfaction. He stepped into the closet and silently closed the door. He liked this part most of all. *It was Showtime!*

§ § §

Clear across town, Sam's pants began to vibrate.

"Damn this thing! How do I turn the ringer on?"

But no one was there to answer him. He fished the phone out of his pants as he drove, nearly running off the road into a parked car. Sam pulled over to the side and punched a few buttons.

First, he read Natalie's email, then Will's text message. A concerned look came over his face. He thought to himself, *Good thing I read the manual on this thing.* Sam pursed his lips together in determination, threw the phone down on the seat and sped away to Natalie's apartment. Despite the fact that he disliked Will Powers, he nonetheless whispered a prayer for him on the way. After all, a cop is a cop, even if you don't like him.

Chapter Forty

"Why is it working so slow! I hate this computer!" Natalie slapped the side of her monitor so hard that she had to quickly reach up and grab it to keep it from falling off onto the floor. It was after midnight and despite the fact that she was the only one in the office, she looked around to make sure no one had seen her. Just 15 more minutes and she would be finished with this incessant Rasco Industrial Kitchen Blender and then she could go sleep on her mother's couch.

"I hate Rasco!"

"Who in the world is Rasco?"

Natalie nearly fell off her chair spinning around so fast.

"Darn it, Jamal, why do you sneak up on me like that. You do that every time I work late!"

The young security guard laughed out loud and leaned one forearm on the top ridge of the cubicle wall.

"Can you believe these ugly, orange cubicles? Why would anyone buy anything so atrocious for an office?"

The hint of a smile played around the corners of Natalie's lips. She shrugged.

"I don't know. You wouldn't see this color in my apartment, that's for sure."

Jamal had short, black hair, beautiful tanned skin, a gold necklace, and his uniform was pressed neatly. Even Natalie had to admit that he was attractive, despite his one-track mind.

"So, that reminds me, Natalie, when are you going to take

me home to see this apartment of yours. You know I'll show you a good time."

Natalie played along with his college-age come-ons. She didn't believe he was a bad person - just stupid for his age.

"I was thinking next Friday would be good."

He nodded.

"Oh yeah. I'm free."

"We could buy a nice bottle of wine, order some takeout, and then snuggle up on the couch together."

Jamal's eyes began to bulge out in anticipation.

"Oh, I'm with ya baby!"

Natalie crossed her legs, allowing her dress to hike up her thigh. She caught his gaze move down toward her bare legs.

"I'm up here, Jamal!"

"Oh yeah! I know! I'm with you!"

"And then we could pop in a movie, turn the lights way down low and watch *Barbie and the Nutcracker*."

Jamal's smile began to fade.

"Barbie and the who?

Natalie nodded.

"Oh yeah. Then my six-year-old daughter, Amethyst could snuggle in between us on the couch and we could have ice cream. The expensive kind with real vanilla flavor!"

Jamal grunted and dropped his arm off the cubicle wall. The wall moved noticeably and Natalie's computer jiggled on the desk in front of her.

"Stop messin' with me, Nat! You know I got the hots for ya. We could work around the kid. I'm a sensitive guy, so long as I get what I need."

Natalie rolled her eyes in disgust.

"No offense, Jamal, you're a good looking boy, but I need a

real man to meet my own needs."

"Oh, baby I could meet your needs just fine. Ain't got no complaints yet!"

Natalie was quick to come back.

"That's not what Erica in shipping and receiving told me."

A full-fledged frown broke across his face like a storm.

"Erica? What did she say about me? I treat her good, man! She didn't say anything to me."

Natalie nodded.

"Now you're getting it, Jamal. Women only complain when they think there's a future. Aside from that, they just quietly move on."

Jamal took one step back as if bombarded with the Kryptonite of truth.

"Yeah, well don't believe everything she says. I gotta go, girl. Gotta make my rounds. You gonna be much longer?"

Natalie swiveled back toward her computer as if the exchange had never occurred.

"I'll be out of here in 15 minutes if you just leave me alone for a bit and let me get my work done."

He waved his hand at her in mock disregard.

"You know you like it. You want me just like the others."

Natalie laughed inside, all the while thinking *That's right, Jamal, I really want to spend a wild evening in the sack so you can be gone by morning and we can act clumsy here at work for the next 5 years.* But she didn't say it out loud.

"Later, Jamal. Have a good night."

The handsome, young security guard moved off down the aisle and was quickly out of sight. Natalie regained her focus and worked to finish her packaging checklist. *I hate checklists. But I have to get home to my Amethyst!* The thought of her little girl spurred her on to work even faster.

§ § §

Jamal swaggered through the empty hallways of the Amanatech Corporation. In his own mind, the whole building belonged to him. During the day it was the realm of the execs, but at night, he became king of the building. He walked past the President's office and peered inside. *Were those miniature Mounds bars in his candy jar?* Jamal stopped. He looked around. To the left. To the right. Then he stepped into the office and scooped up one for himself. The Executives had all the best candy. He walked around the desk with his ill-gotten gain and plopped himself down in the high-backed leather chair. He propped his feet up on the desk, all the while being careful not to disturb the papers on the left side of the oak top. This guy kept his desk really clean and organized. Jamal thought to himself, *Someday my desk will be like this. I'll finish college, get a job, buy a fancy car and bring babes back to my condo.* And then he thought, *And maybe, if she's lucky, I just might hire Natalie as my Secretary. She's a good looking woman ... for her age.*

He accidently dropped the empty Mounds wrapper on the carpet and quickly leaned over to pick it up. Best not leave any evidence. And when he looked up, he was surprised to see a man in a dark ski mask pointing the funny looking pistol at his face.

His blood turned to ice with fear. Jamal heard the suppressed shot, saw the smoke rise up, and felt the shock wave as the bullet slammed into his head. Oddly enough, his last thought was, *I shouldn't have taken the Mounds bar.*

Chapter Forty-One

Sam Colton looked down at Will's body and bile moved up into his throat. He had been mutilated almost beyond recognition with a kitchen knife. Sam could never get used to the sight and smell of dead bodies, especially when they were carved up, and especially when he knew the victim. In Vietnam he'd gotten used to it, at least for a time. It was a survival mechanism he was sure, but the feelings always came back to him after a firefight. The feelings of revulsion, of remorse, and ... of guilt, either misplaced or merited.

Quickly, he pushed down the bile and threw a switch inside his brain that turned off his emotions. It was another survival mechanism he'd trained himself to do over the decades. He remembered the day he'd retired from the force, and his thoughts, *I'll never have to see another dead body again. The next dead body will be mine.* Right about now, he wished he could trade places with Will, wished he could be done with this life and all the crap it threw at you.

He looked up at the ceiling just to give himself a break from the horror of Will's bloody body. The life-sized picture of Natalie was taped securely and the word "SINNER" was scrawled in red marker across her face. Along with the word was a squiggle through her face.

"What does that mark mean?

The photographer looked up at him.

"I've seen it before. My wife's an editor and she uses them

all the time. That's a proofer's mark."

Sam nodded.

"What does it mean?"

"It means *delete*."

"Get a picture of that too. And this as well."

Sam stepped aside and let the photographer do his job. He moved into the back of the bedroom and opened the closet door. He could still see the imprints in the carpet where the man had been standing. Sam knelt down and looked closer. They were big, maybe size 13. He took one of Natalie's shoes and placed it next to the imprint. They didn't match by a long shot.

"Neal, get a picture of this imprint in the carpet. Make it a close up. And have Phil check for fibers on the carpet in here too."

"Lighten up, Sam. I know how to do my job!"

Sam nodded.

"Yeah, sorry, Neal. I know that. Just a little bit involved about this one."

Neal looked up from his camera.

"I thought you didn't like Will? He sure didn't like you. He made no bones about it either. Heck, no one liked Will. He was a jerk!"

Sam stood up and stepped out of the closet.

"Yeah, I know, but we're all cops, even the jerks. It's a brotherhood. And you can pick your friends, but you're stuck with your relatives."

Neal moved over and knelt down beside the closet door before snapping another picture.

"Yeah, well, I suppose you're right, Sam. I just didn't like the guy. He had a way of getting under my skin. Ya know what

I mean?"

"Yeah. I know."

But Sam was deep in thought now. There was no vanilla latte and no DNA sample. Either this wasn't the Vanilla Killer, or Will had surprised him and this wasn't a planned murder. Honestly, Sam didn't know which scenario was more true. For all he knew, this could be a burglary unrelated to the case, but he didn't think so. Sam looked down at his watch. It was almost midnight.

"Have the feds been here yet?"

"No, not yet. We called them though."

Sam started to walk toward the door out to the living room.

"I gotta go check on something now. Who's coming in from forensics?"

Neal looked up a bit confused.

"I already told you that. It's Phil. He should be here any minute."

Sam nodded.

"Oh, yeah, that's right. I remember now. Please have him call me when he's done, okay?"

"Yeah, sure thing, Sam. You okay?"

Sam pasted a smile onto his face and nodded as he left the room. He went down to his car and sat there for a few minutes, just thinking. He pulled out his Blackberry and scanned for messages and emails. Nothing. Then he went back and re-read Natalie's last message.

Sam,

Have to work very late tonight. Amethyst is at my Mom's. All is well. I'll stay there tonight. Keep your powder dry.

Natalie

Out of habit, he looked at his watch again and thought to himself. *Too late to call. I shouldn't bother them this late.*

Sam hesitated, then buckled up his seat belt, started the car and threw it into gear. No harm in just checking though. He wasn't going to sleep tonight anyway, so he might as well make sure she got home okay. At that moment his mind drifted off to his daughter and grand daughter far away in another state. They still hadn't returned his calls. Perhaps ... But Sam quickly brushed the paranoid thought out of his head. They were okay. He was sure of it. And Natalie was okay too. He just had to check. He had to be sure. It was the parent part of him that he had to satisfy. Or maybe it was the soldier part, or the cop part. He didn't even know anymore. He just knew that he had to make sure Natalie and Amethyst were okay or he wouldn't get any sleep tonight.

And right about now, he desperately wanted sleep, wanted the respite from the present, but ... most of all, even more than sleep or food or even the breath of life, he wanted to catch the bastard who was killing his people.

Chapter Forty-Two

"Yes!"

Natalie quickly logged out of her computer and bent down to scoop up her purse underneath the desk. She looked up at the clock to the left of her monitor: 12:13AM. She saw the picture of Amethyst beside the clock and smiled. *Finally, I can go home and see my little girl sleeping!*

Then she remembered, *I forgot to fill out my timecard.* She hesitated, just for a moment and then stood up to leave. *Forget it! It can wait until morning!* And then the thought occurred to her, *It's already morning.*

As she walked away, she glanced over at Mark's desk and shivered. At least he'd gone home hours ago. He gave her the creeps more than ever now. She reached down into the back compartment of her purse and felt the solid grip of her pistol. It was a reassuring thing to her, an ever-present help in time of trouble. Normally she'd been carrying it in a belly-band holster underneath her clothes, but a few hours ago after everyone else had gone home, she'd walked into the bathroom stall and moved it to a more readily accessible place. Not wanting to run into Jamal again, she took the long way out to the elevator. The last thing she wanted was to be slowed down by some boy-man, sex-god wannabe when she was trying to get home to her kid.

Natalie looked at her marble reflection on the fancy walls as she walked down the hallway towards the main elevator. She was surprised to see the reflection of a frowning woman, mouth pursed tightly together, and eyes filled with tension. She was fast approaching middle-aged. And then she thought to herself, *How does anyone know when they're middle-aged?* After all, in order to know the middle of your life, then you also have to know when your life is ending. It occurred to her that middle-aged for some people is 21 or 40 or 7 or even 52.

She stopped in front of the elevator door and pushed the down button. She winced as the bell sounded loudly in the vacuous, empty halls of the deserted building. Jamal was sure to hear that and head her off at the pass. Maybe she should have taken the stairs. But it was too late. The door opened right away. She glanced both directions quickly and then rushed inside. Natalie turned around and faced the doors before pushing the lit-up "1" button on the panel in front of her. The door closed and the elevator began to move slowly.

And then she looked down to her right, as if by an afterthought, and saw the paper cup on the floor in the corner. It was white, with green logo and lettering. It said *Starbuck's.* A confused look swept over Natalie's face, and, more by instinct than anything else, she bent down to take a closer look at the cup. She saw a little puff of steam come out the hole in the top so she touched the cardboard and felt it was still hot. She wondered to herself, *How long do those little jackets keep the coffee warm?*

And then she noticed the bold printing on the side of the cup. She rotated it around and saw the following words written in black felt marker:

"Hello Alice - Drink Me!"

The brow of Natalie's forehead furled into a myriad of lines and creases.

"What the ... "

And then the elevator jerked to a halt and Natalie fell off to one side, catching herself with her right hand on the floor. Quickly, she stood back up and started pressing the "1" button on the elevator control panel over and over again. But nothing happened and that dark, sick feeling in the pit of her stomach began to rise up, taking shape and form. Her hand moved instinctively inside her purse and wrapped around the butt of her pistol. She gripped it tightly and waited.

Chapter Forty-Three

The curb loomed up quickly and Sam stepped on the brakes, bringing his truck to a halt about 100 feet south of the driveway. He looked up into the second floor and saw lights. The clock on his dashboard said 12:16 AM. A flicker of hope lit up his countenance. Perhaps Natalie had just gotten here from work. He didn't really need to talk to her, he just wanted to know that she was okay before he went to bed. Then he looked around but couldn't find her car in the driveway. Reaching up, Sam disconnected the dome light before opening the door and stepping out onto the pavement. He reached up under his left armpit to feel the solid mass of his 357 revolver. After taking one last look around, Sam moved quietly off the pavement and onto the grassy lawn. The neon streetlight lit up the neighborhood in an eerie glow just enough for him to move without a flashlight. He peered through the garage window and could make out the silhouette of a car, but it was not Natalie's.

For a moment, he stood beside the garage in indecision. Someone was awake, probably her mother, and normally he would just knock on the door, but ... he just didn't feel comfortable around the old woman. She always looked at him like a bear eyeing a piece of hanging meat. On the other hand, her mother would have information that he needed about where Natalie was and when was the last time she'd heard from her. But he didn't want to go in there this late unless he had to.

Sam stuck his left hand down into his pants pocket to fish out his Blackberry. He found the right button and pushed it, causing the brightness of the screen to light up the night, blinding his eyes for several seconds. He tried to cover the light with his hand, but to no avail. After finding the right button, Sam pushed it and waited while the phone rang. Finally, Natalie answered.

"Sam! I'm trapped in the elevator. Something's wrong! He's here! He's coming for me!"

Sam tried to stay calm in his response.

"Just calm down, Natalie, and tell me where you are."

"I'm at work. I'm trapped in the elevator and someone is coming down through the hatch in the ceiling. I hear them unscrewing it."

Sam's mind raced as he talked.

"Do you have your pistol?"

"Yes!"

"Good! Here's what I want you to do."

But before Sam could utter his next words, the heavy, steel shovel came down on the back of his head, rendering him useless. The Blackberry fell to the soft, green grass and continued to glow in the night.

""Sam! Where are you? What should I do? Talk to me!"

The man in the hooded sweatshirt laughed out loud as he picked up the cell phone and spoke into it.

"Sam can't come to the phone right now, but if you'll leave a message, he'll get back to you."

And then the laughing started to crescendo until it built to a crazy fervor.

"Not really, Natalie. Sam is going to die. I'm executing him for crimes against humanity. And then I'm going into your mother's house to interrogate your little girl. I'm pretty sure your mom is going to die too, so I hope there's nothing unsaid between you and your mother. It's so sad when parents and kids don't get along. And as for Amethyst, well, I just might have a more righteous need of her than you do. I might let her live, but we'll just have to see. I think I can still purge the evil from her, but I'm not making any promises."

Natalie pressed her back against the corner of the elevator as the cell connection went dead in her hand. Only one thing blazed through her mind, *My daughter! I have to save her. I have to get out of here.* And then she thought, *That voice, where have I heard that voice?*

Four feet away, the vented door above her fell onto the elevator floor and clattered to a stop. She saw two feet drop down through the ceiling and hang there above her. Natalie drew her pistol and waited for the rest of the body to follow. As soon as she saw the kill zone, she was ready to pull the trigger.

Chapter Forty-Four

When Sam Colton came to, his head throbbed and felt like a lead weight. He tried to jump to his feet, but soon discovered that duct tape bound his hands and legs securely. He wiggled back and forth but only succeeded in chafing his skin. Everything was still black and he could feel duct tape over his eyes and wrapped tightly around his forehead.

"Why good morning, Officer Colton. How are you feeling this evening? How's the head?"

Sam moved himself to a sitting position on the floor, using his forehead to push against the wall. He felt carpet beneath him and cold air from the air conditioner coming out of the floor register. For some reason his surroundings felt familiar. Sam snapped back at him with an edge in his voice.

"It hurts like hell! What did you hit me with?"

The man smiled but Sam couldn't see it.

"It was just a garden shovel. I seldom bring weapons with me when I commit felonies. Being a law enforcement officer, I'm sure you understand why. Besides, why trouble myself when every house I enter is jam packed with weapons of every shape and size." There was silence for a moment. "Especially your house Sam. You've got a regular arsenal in here." Sam thought to himself *He moved me! I'm tied up in my own office. I recognize the smell of gun oil.* "But, of course, I have a weapon now, a 357 magnum revolver. It's a nice piece, very reliable with lots of knock-down power. Stainless steel too. Not one of those super light titanium jobs they make now days that hurt your hand every time you pull the trigger. And so many people go in for those fancy, semi-automatics these days, with their high-capacity magazines and fancy frangible rounds. The business of killing is becoming way too complicated. I liked it better in the old days when you could just cut people up and be done with it. But now, people are carrying guns, trying to defend themselves, it just makes my job that much harder. It's not very considerate of them. Don't you agree?"

Sam thought for a moment, *Keep him talking. Keep him talking so he doesn't kill you. Let him bond to you, that way you are no longer an object that is easily dispatched.*

"I suppose it's all a matter of perspective. You and I have the same job, we just operate from opposite points of view."

There was silence for a moment as Sam waited for a reply.

"Yes, perspective. I suppose that's one way of putting it. We both deal with sin, crime as you would call it. I guess the difference is that I'm much more effective than you are. Let's face it, the criminal justice system is anything but efficient these days. Why, in the time it takes you to catch one bad, guy and convict him, I can dole out justice to dozens of sinners. I like my way better, no offense intended."

"None taken. Different strokes, I suppose."

Sam waited again for the clumsy silence to break. He knew better than to push the man. He heard something hard slide across a table top, then a sigh and the placing of a mug back down onto the table. It was then that he smelled the coffee.

"What are you drinking?"

There was the sound of soft laughter.

"You tell me, Mr. Colton. After all, you're the Detective."

Sam thought for a moment before answering. He knew he

was being tested and felt instinctively that in order to live a bit longer he had to perform well. He had to impress his captor.

"Coffee, extra strong, home-brewed I think, one maybe two spoons of sugar. I don't smell any cream." Sam paused a moment before continuing. "There's something else too. Something light, something that I can't quite place ... Vanilla!"

He heard the sound of light clapping.

"Bravo, Mr. Colton. You get an A plus!"

"Do your sons drink vanilla coffee as well?"

There was silence for a moment.

"Impressive, Mr. Colton. You really are a detective aren't you. You already know about my sons. What else do you know?"

Sam forced himself to smile.

"Let's not talk about that quite yet, but all in due time. I figure I've got until morning before you kill me, assuming it fits your timetable and I'm interesting enough."

"That's true, Mr. Colton. After all, no one likes a boring conversationalist. People just don't talk like they used to. Most people don't even know their own neighbors. It's sad, really. The world used to be a better place to live. You agree?"

Sam nodded slightly despite his blindness.

"Without a doubt. So, do Mark and Kayne both drink vanilla flavor in their coffee?"

"You are a really smart man, Mr. Colton, and I like that. When I spoke with Kayne several hours ago, he warned me about your cleverness. Kayne liked you, which is quite unusual to say the least. He's a pretty good judge of character. I think I like you too, so far."

Sam didn't say anything. He just waited. Somehow, he had to keep the guy talking, giving him information. So long as he was talking, then he wasn't killing anyone.

"But I'm being rude. Let me answer your question as best I can. Kayne doesn't drink coffee at all. He hates it, says it's too bitter. Not a big deal. Though he has a taste for other unnamed vices which we may discuss later on. Now, Mark, on the other hand, that's a more complex answer. You see, a part of Mark loves coffee, loves to taste it, to feel it, to swish it around on his tongue before swallowing. It's the way I brought him up, I suppose. I just find linear personalities to be tedious and one sin I can never forgive is boorishness. You have to admit, Sam, that my sons, whatever else you may think about them, they are very interesting and colorful characters. Wouldn't you agree?"

Sam smiled on the inside. *He just called me by my first name. I'm making headway.*

§ § §

The man's heavy boots dropped down onto the elevator floor with a loud thud and Natalie screamed as loud as she could.

"Jamal! Jamal! Help me!"

The man rose up from the floor and laughed softly to himself. He wore a black ski mask and carried a bowie knife in his right hand.

"Shut up, Natalie! You're hurting my ears!"

"Don't move or I'll shoot!"

The man leaned his head back and roared with laughter.

"Why do people always say that? It's hilarious! I mean look at it my way, Natalie. Someone tells me to stop or they'll shoot. What does that really mean to me? What does it tell me? It tells me that you're not likely to shoot. It tells me that you're paralyzed with fear. It tells me that you have a conscience and you don't want to really shoot at all. So why say things that you don't mean? Can't we just be honest with one another, Natalie? Honesty is so important in a relationship don't you think?"

Natalie stopped screaming and extended the pistol out in front of her chest so it almost touched the man. Then she realized her mistake and pulled it back in closer to her body so he couldn't grab it. She recognized Mark's voice, but not the tone.

"Mark, I'll shoot you. I really will. I swear to God I'll shoot you and leave you to die alone in this elevator."

The man leaned back against the elevator wall and folded his arms across his chest.

"Just so you know, Jamal's dead. I left him in the President's office. Caught him stealing candy. That is so disgusting. Why didn't he just buy his own Mounds bar? People just have no respect for other people's property these days. Am I the only one who finds that disturbing?"

He waited for Natalie to answer, but the realization that Jamal was dead and that he would not be helping her sank in to her core and turned to silent terror in her chest.

"What's the matter, Nat? Cat got your tongue?"

He raised the 10-inch knife up to his chest and held the shiny blade to the light.

"Do you like my new knife, Natalie? I bought it special just to kill you. You should feel honored. I've never treated anyone so special before." He paused a moment. "Are you grateful, Natalie? Do you appreciate the work I've put into this evening? I have worked so long and hard to bring us together."

Natalie moved her head back and forth in denial.

"No, I don't appreciate it at all, Mark, and I wish you'd just crawl back up through that hole and go away."

He shook his head and laughed out loud.

"You still don't get it, do you Natalie? You're not dealing with Mark anymore. Mark isn't here. He's probably home crying and sobbing like a little baby. He's so weak! I can't stand that little terd! I've spent my whole life bailing him out of trouble, propping him up, making him strong. It's almost a full-time job, actually. Did you know that we are twins? I'm the big brother, older by 3 minutes, so I guess it's my job to take care of my baby brother. But his weakness just nauseates me sometimes. I mean really! He's quite obviously the runt of the litter!"

Natalie's mind reeled with questions and uncertainty. *Did Mark really have a twin brother, an evil twin? Was he going to kill her? Was Jamal really dead? Where is Sam? Is he on his way to help?* Finally, Natalie spoke.

"But ... your voice, it sounds just like Mark's. How can you not be him?"

The man shrugged.

"Hasn't that boy told you anything about me? I'm hurt! After all I've done for him and he keeps me a secret like I'm some stranger on the streets?"

Natalie tightened her grip on the pistol.

"He doesn't talk much."

The man laughed again.

"That's the understatement of the year! I keep forgetting how quiet he is. The man hardly says a word. But that's okay, we have time to talk for a while. Let me fill you in so that we can get better acquainted. My name is Kayne, and Mark and I are twins, but not identical twins. We're fraternal twins, and that means that we don't look like each other. We don't come from the same egg at all, just the same womb at the same time.

I can see why some people get confused by it. But I can assure you that I really am Mark's brother."

Natalie didn't flinch but just kept holding the pistol out in front close to her sternum.

"Fraternal twins don't have the same voice. You're Mark. I can tell. I know your voice."

The man shook his head back and forth as if in disgust. He reached up and grabbed the top of his ski mask with his left hand and pulled. The cap slid up over his face and off the top of his head with ease.

"See, Natalie. I'm not Mark. I'm Kayne. Can't you see?"

Chapter Forty-Five

"I don't really know that much about them. I spoke with Kayne once and I've read his file, but I know very little about Mark aside from what Kayne told me. What's he like?"

The old man leaned back in the wooden chair and crossed his left leg onto his right.

"That's interesting, so what exactly did Kayne tell you about his brother?"

Oddly enough, Sam found himself wanting to reach up and scratch his chin while he recalled the conversation, but his hands were bound tightly at the wrists.

"I believe his exact words were, *I hate that little freak!*"

Sam heard the man chuckling softly.

"Yes, well, they are brothers. I'm afraid they've always felt this sort of sibling rivalry between each other. I don't know why, vying for daddy's affection perhaps. I certainly didn't foster it. I always tried to get them to work together as a family, but they never would. Family is so important, don't you think so too, Sam?"

Sam hesitated and the man picked up on it right away.

"Oh, I see, family must be a sore spot for you."

Despite his lack of sight, Sam turned and looked toward the wall.

"Oh my. Sam has problems at home doesn't he? Hmmm, can't be the wife. She's been dead for years. Only one child, a daughter, lives in Akron, Ohio. Address is 1274 Fulton Avenue. Phone number is 330-43 ...”

Something inside Sam snapped and he lashed out in anger at the unseen man.

“Shut up! Leave my daughter out of this! Just leave my family alone!”

The man smiled an unseen grin before feigning sympathy.

“I’m sorry, Sam. I didn’t know it was such a sensitive issue. I should have been more careful. I should have thought better of it. I mean, yes, we’re both fathers and it would hurt me too if my sons hadn’t called me in months and if they had cut off all contact with me. I can’t for the life of me figure out what would cause a daughter to do a thing like that. Can you, Sam?”

Sam didn’t say anything. His head sagged down onto his chest.

“How could she hurt you like that, Sam. How could she do a thing like that?” The man took another sip of his coffee. “To be a parent is to hurt. The kids are all so disappointing. Listen, I can relate to you and I’m not at all unsympathetic with your plight. Neither of my sons really turned out according to my plans as well.” He shrugged. “Free will, I suppose. They just pretty much do whatever they want. I thought for sure if I disciplined them, gave them clothes, food, put a roof over their heads, that they would honor me, but ... life is full of little disappointments I suppose.”

Sam struggled to regain his composure. His life was in the balance as well as Natalie’s and those of Amethyst and her mother. He had to stay calm, had to lower his heart rate and prevent the adrenaline surge.

“I’d rather not talk about it if you don’t mind. It’s very personal for me. And like you said, it’s a sore spot.”

The man nodded his head in understanding.

"Hmm, well, normally I would respect your privacy and give you some space, but ... you see, Sam, I'm usually a very nice person, but, I have this weakness in my personality that just has to intrude on other people's secrets. It's a hobby of mine. I collect stories, trophies, other little tidbits of a private nature."

Sam's head rose up off his chest and an attitude of defiance pursed his lips together tightly.

"My family is not a trophy and it's none of your damned business!"

The old man smiled and patiently took another sip of his coffee. He nodded in understanding.

"Sure, Sam. I understand. And I respect that, it's just that it's pathological and I can't really stop myself. I want to know. I NEED to know!" His voice was beginning to rise now. "And if you don't tell me all about your daughter and her little girl, then I'm walking into the other room. Then I'll very calmly bring Amethyst in here with you. I'll remove your blindfold, and then ... I'll rape her to within an inch of her life."

§ § §

Natalie's heart was racing as the ski mask came off and left Mark's face in plain view. Her eyes squinted together and she pressed her back harder against the elevator wall behind her. Oddly enough, the sight of wimpy Mark's face had a calming effect on her. She knew he was a coward. She knew it because she had stood up to him before. In the privacy of her own thoughts she remembered the time he had wet his pants in the parking lot when she'd pointed her gun at him. Natalie glanced down at his pants, but they were dry.

"Do you see, now, Natalie? I'm not Mark. I'm Kayne!"

Natalie found her head nodding up and down with little or no conscious effort. She drew a quick conclusion: This may be Mark's body, but it is not Mark inside of him. But Natalie didn't say that out loud. She kept it to herself. When she spoke again, her voice had become surprisingly calm.

"Yes, I can see that now. You are different from Mark. The last time I pointed a gun at Mark he wet his pants, but you don't even look afraid. That's weird. Aren't you concerned I might pull the trigger?"

The man looked over at her and smiled as he tested the edge of the knife on his thumb.

"No, not really." And then he laughed. "You see, Natalie, I'm not afraid, because I was in your apartment last night and took the bullets out of your gun as you slept."

And then his laugh crescendoed to a higher pitch. This time it seemed more diabolical than before and it sent chills up and down Natalie's spine. She struggled to keep her newfound calm, but she was losing the battle. All she wanted to do was to check the cylinder to see if he was lying. Her one and only thought was, *Are there any bullets in my gun?* He took a step forward.

"Now give me the gun, Natalie! Just give it to me!"

Natalie held on to it even tighter and put a little more pressure on the trigger.

"Give it up you little witch! It's no good to you anyway! Just give it to me before I stab you!"

Just as he raised up the knife and stepped forward, Natalie pulled the trigger.

§ § §

Sam's scream was like that of a caged animal, thoughtless

and out of control.

"Leave her alone! Leave the little girl alone!"

"Tell me, Sam. Give me what I want! I want to know everything from her shoe size all the way down to what color panties she wears!"

Sam tried to control himself, but all he felt was rage and the desire to strangle the man. Sam had killed many men, but this was the first life he truly longed to take.

"If you touch Amethyst I'll kill you! I'll rip you apart with my bare hands! Don't you dare hurt her!"

But it was too late. Sam's heart sunk as the office door slammed behind his captor. His only thought was, *He didn't even give me a chance to talk. He wants to rape her!*

§ § §

The hammer on Natalie's gun came down with a loud, metallic "Click". Her panic heightened and she pulled the trigger again. Click! An empty chamber had never sounded so loud. By now he was a step closer. Click! And then he was beside her. Click!

His knife came down and sank into the flesh of Natalie's right bicep, sending her pistol clattering benignly to the floor. Natalie screamed and rushed into the corner and cowered there with her back to him. She reached into her purse and pulled out her cell phone but he was already coming at her again. She felt the knife stab into her left shoulder and the cell phone crashed to the elevator floor in pieces.

"No! No! Please! Don't kill me!"

And then Mark backed away and started to smile again.

"Now see, Natalie. That wasn't so hard now was it? Now we have a proper relationship. Now the pecking order has been established and we can move on with the proper relationship."

He looked down and saw the blood on the blade of his knife and his eyes glistened when he saw it.

"I could have killed you so easily, Natalie. It would have been easy. I've killed dozens of people with blades."

Natalie felt the warmth of blood flowing down the sleeve of her blouse. No arteries were severed.

"I was very careful to penetrate only an inch or so and to miss the arteries. It's a question of experience and self control. To be quite frank with you, 10 years ago I wouldn't have been able to control myself. I would have just plunged in the knife as deep as it went and then ripped and shredded everything in its path. Ten years ago you'd already be dead."

He hesitated a moment, and then his smile changed. He took a step forward as Natalie cringed and whimpered in the corner.

"No, no, don't be afraid, Natalie. I'm not going to hurt you. I'm not going to hurt you! I love you, Natalie! What happened! Who did this to you?"

Natalie looked at him with a mixture of disbelief and terror in her eyes. Mark looked down and saw the huge knife in his right hand. He dropped it to the floor and it fell with a clang.

"Natalie, let me help you."

He walked over to the control panel wall and opened the steel door that said "First Aid". He took out the plastic box, laid it on the floor beside her and opened it up.

"I'm sorry about my brother. Did Kayne do this to you? He did, didn't he?"

Natalie didn't answer. Her whole body trembled as she lay there on the floor bleeding. Mark took out a gauze pad and some adhesive tape, then he knelt beside her and gently tore the sleeve off her blouse and pulled it carefully down over her wrist. Natalie eyed the knife three feet away in the opposite corner, wondering, *Can I get to it in time?*

"I was hoping if I didn't let you out of my sight that I could protect you, but Kayne is a very tough and smart man. I only lost sight of you for just a few minutes and look what he's done!"

He pressed the gauze pad around her bicep and held it there with lots of pressure. Natalie could feel the power behind his touch, suddenly realizing that he could break her with one fit of rage. Then he wrapped the tape around her arm securing the pad in place.

"Just press down hard until the bleeding stops, and then you'll be okay."

Mark gently took her left hand and placed it on top of the gauze.

"See. Like this. It's easy."

And then he noticed blood coming from her left shoulder as well.

"Damn him! He got you up there as well." He shook his head from side to side. "I'm surprised he let you live. Thank god I got here in time to stop him. But you're going to be okay, Natalie. I promise you. I'm going to get you out of here and I won't let you out of my sight until my brother is caught. I shouldn't have let him get this far. I should have turned him in a long time ago."

His hands moved up to the bloody and torn blouse on her shoulder. He ripped part of it away and then dabbed at the gash with some of the gauze roll.

"This one looks bad, but at least it's not deep. You're going to be okay."

Gently, like a parent nurturing a hurt child, Mark took to nursing her wound. When he finished, he leaned his back against the wall and slumped down on the floor beside her.

Natalie began to shake and then she lowered her head down onto her chest and cried out loud. A bit of drool flowed from her mouth and dripped onto her chest as tears came down her cheeks.

"Natalie, what's wrong? I'm here now. You're going to be okay! I'm going to save you and then we can be happy. Don't you see? It's all okay now."

But Natalie continued to cry. Mark felt clumsy and didn't know what to do. So he just sat there and folded his hands in his lap as she cried.

Chapter Forty-Six

Sam's mind raced out of control and his heart rate sky-rocketed. *He's going to kill Amethyst!* But then his training and years of experience kicked in. *Gain control! Analyze the situation. Make a plan! Save Amethyst. Get Natalie!*

Gradually, Sam's heart rate began to lower and his mind began to clear. *Set priorities. What do I have to do first? What is my situation?*

He thought for a moment. *I'm in my office study. I'm bound with duct tape. There's a killer in the house. He's going to rape and kill Amethyst.*

In a whisper he said, *Remove the duct tape.* And then he took mental note of all that was in his study and what was within reach. *Scissors, pocket knife, letter opener.* All on his desk where the man had been sitting.

Sam rotated around with his back to the wall and inched himself to the desk, but when he tried to raise himself up, his movement was stopped by a cord that connected his wrists and his ankles. He'd been hog tied! Sam groaned in disappointment, but quickly went back to thinking.

"What can I reach?"

And then it came to him and he pushed himself along the floor until he reached the desk lamp cord hanging down to the floor. Sam reached his hands up until his fingers wrapped around the electrical cord, and then he gave it a jerk. All he got was slack. He released the cord and moved his hands up again and took another grip on the cord. He jerked it down again and felt the heavy desk lamp crash down on his head.

For a moment there was a new kind of blackness, but then his mind quickly came to again and all he could feel was the lump on the side of his head and some liquid that he knew must be blood. Just as he'd hoped, the glass globe of the lamp had shattered on the floor all around him. Slowly, he pushed himself forward and ran his hands across the carpet until a sharp pain stabbed into the back side of his middle finger. He jerked away but then moved back slower, this time probing for the piece of broken glass. Once he had it in his hand, he realized it was too small and he continued searching. He found several other shards, cutting his fingers each time. Finally, he found the right length and placed it in his fingers with the sharp end pointing down and moved it up and down across the duct tape. To his surprise, the duct tape sliced through cleanly.

A smile moved across his unseeing face as he thought to himself. *What is my next priority?* The answer came back quick and obvious. *Regain my sight.*

Quickly, he unwrapped the cut strands of tape from his wrists, which proved to be difficult because they were slippery with his own blood. As soon as his hands were completely free, he reached up to the duct tape on his face. Sam froze and his heart raced again. Something metal was pressing against the back of his neck

"I have to admit, Officer Colton, that was very impressive. I'm so glad I got to watch it firsthand."

And then Sam's body jerked and spasmed as 50,000 volts of electricity slammed into his body at the speed of light. His teeth clenched and he screamed involuntarily as the electrons invaded his body and rendered him helpless once more. A few seconds later the pain stopped.

"You see I very seldom bring weapons with me when I'm committing a felony, but in your case, Sam, I made an exception."

The pain started again and Sam screamed rigidly on the floor until it stopped.

"Sam, did you know that there is a common misconception about the voltage of Tasers. Yes they are a whopping 50,000 volts but that's only to make the initial contact between the electric probes and the skin. Once the contact is made, the voltage drops to about 1,300 volts at about 18 pulses per second. The voltage has nothing to do with the strength of the Taser or any stun gun. High voltage with low amperage won't kill you. But it sure does hurt like hell doesn't it?"

He pushed the button again and Sam's body jerked and spasmed on the carpet. He was as helpless as a baby.

$$\mathit{\S}\ \mathit{\S}\ \mathit{\S}$$

Mark got up and walked over to the gun on the elevator floor. He picked it up and stepped back over to Natalie. He knelt back down and placed the pistol into her bloody hand.

"You can trust me, Natalie. I want you to know that. I want you to know how much I love you and that I'm going to always take care of you."

He sat down beside her and sighed.

"Yes, I know you've been through a lot. Some guy tried to rape you and you killed him. Then my brother stabbed you. But you have to accentuate the positive! You're okay now! I'm here with you and you're going to be okay. But you have to trust me, Natalie."

Natalie picked her head up and looked into Mark's eyes.

They were pleading and sincere and she couldn't help but wonder how he'd gotten this way. Then her mind flashed back to Sam and to her daughter, Amethyst, and her mother. He had given her the gun, but what she really needed was the knife. And then a very important thought came into her mind, *What would Sam Colton do?* The answer came back loud and clear.

"Yes, I can see that now, Mark. Thank you for saving me. I'm so sorry we couldn't have lunch together. I really screwed up and I'm sorry."

Mark's face appeared to beam uncontrollably.

"Really?"

Natalie nodded her head.

"It's just that, like you said, things have been so hard for me lately. I've been so confused and scared. Sometimes a girl just doesn't know who to turn to. Do you know what I mean?"

Mark smiled and nodded his head.

"Yes, I do know what you mean. The world is cruel and unrighteous, and a person has to be strong to survive. Everyone has to have a strong friend to protect them, and I want to be that strong person for you."

And then a faraway look came into his eyes and Natalie watched with impatient curiosity.

"The people who were supposed to protect me ... they didn't. They hurt me instead, so I had to find a friend who was strong and brave. He got me through the hard times, but now I don't need him anymore. I don't even want him. I'm strong on my own now and I won't let him come back to hurt me or you."

And then his eyes looked into Natalie's and she got the distinct impression that he was going to cry.

"I'm a big boy now, Natalie, and no one is ever going to

hurt me again!"

Inside her mind Natalie repeated the same mantra, *What would Sam Colton do? Focus! Focus! Focus!*

"Yes, Mark. You are strong. And I need your help. I need you so much. Will you please help me now? Can you get me out of this elevator?"

Mark's face lit up as if the idea had just occurred to him for the first time.

"Yeah! That's a good idea! I can do that! I'm a big boy now!"

He looked around the elevator as if assessing the situation. He saw the broken cell phone, then his eyes lit up and he moved over to the control panel wall. Mark opened the door that said *Emergency Phone*, and put the receiver to his ear. After quite a few seconds, he frowned.

"No one is answering."

Natalie thought to herself, *That's because you killed the security guard for stealing a Mounds bar*, but she kept her thoughts to herself.

"Do you have your cell phone, Mark?"

"Yes! Of course! My cell phone! I always have it with me."

He reached up into the cell phone holder on his belt and turned back to her with a confused look on his face.

"I wonder where it went."

He got up and starting pushing buttons on the control panel but none of them seemed to work. Mark looked down at her again.

"You're losing too much blood. I have to get you out of here fast!"

Natalie nodded.

"Yes, please hurry. Can you get up the elevator shaft to the next floor and call for help?"

A smile swept across his face and stayed there, like a little boy who'd just gotten a new puppy.

"I'll be right back, Natalie."

Mark put his right foot up onto the railing but hesitated and brought it back down. He knelt and scooped up the big knife on the floor and placed it back in the sheath on his belt.

"Natalie, be careful, and if my brother comes back, I want you to ..."

Mark leaned his head down and gently kissed her on top of the head.

"Don't feel bad about what has to be done. All unrighteousness has to be purged. You have to protect yourself and your little girl. "

Natalie nodded and then he stood up and climbed on out of the elevator. After his legs disappeared through the ceiling, his head popped back down through the hatch.

"Don't worry. I'll be back!"

Chapter Forty-Seven

When Sam Colton regained consciousness, he was sitting upright in a chair and he was bound tightly with enough duct tape to secure a grizzly bear. But the tape was off his eyes and he could see again.

"You see, Sam, I've been commissioned by God to purge the world of all unrighteousness, which, quite frankly is a bigger task than I thought it would be, which is why God has given me special powers and special sanction. God has always been that way. It's recorded in the Bible."

The old man had gray, thinning hair and he wore a simple work shirt and faded blue jeans. His back was hunched over as he worked to bind Amethyst to the top of Sam's office desk. The little, blonde-haired girl appeared to be sleeping or unconscious and wore handcuffs on both wrists and ankles. The man stretched out Amethyst's left arm, placing it flat on the desk top. Then he picked up the hammer and spike. Sam cringed when he saw it.

"Don't worry, Sam. I'm not going to hurt her. I'm not a barbarian, you know."

"He placed the spike through the metal link in the handcuff chain and pounded it down into the oak desk top until the nail head was flush with the wood. He repeated the procedure with her right hand and them with both her legs. He turned to Sam and spoke softly.

"It's okay. I've done this before."

That's when Sam noticed the red pin cushion with metal needles jutting up in all directions. He recognized it as belonging to his wife, Sandy. The old man must have found it in her sewing stuff. Sam had never thrown away any of her things. Her clothes were still in the closet.

"What are you going to do to her?"

The old man stood up and stretched his back and put the hammer down on the desk beside the unconscious girl.

"I used to do this without sedative, but they wiggled too much and then I had to do it all over again. That's what happened to Mark. He would just never hold still long enough for me to be precise in my work."

Sam couldn't take his eyes off the needles.

"What are those needles for?"

The old man smiled.

"I told you that the Lord has given me special powers and special sanction, but along with all that, he's given me special knowledge as well. I can heal the girl. God showed me how."

The old man reached down and carefully selected a sewing needle about two inches long. He held it up to the light as if examining it.

"What are you going to do to her?"

"I have to purge the evil. It's located in her frontal lobe. Once I pierce it with this holy sword, it will be forced to leave her. Because evil cannot coexist with righteousness, just as light cannot exist with darkness. It's in the Bible you know."

Sam strained against the duct tape but it wouldn't budge. He yelled as loud as he could.

"Stop it! Stop it right now!"

The old man looked over at him and smiled.

"I can't stop, Sam. It's for her own good. The Lord has

commanded it."

The veins stuck out in Sam's throat as he strained against his bonds.

"Damn it, Jerry, don't you see that this is mad? Can't you see that God is love and that he would never command you to do this to a child?"

Jerry smiled.

"Now, Sam, that's the first time you've used my real name. Why were you holding that back from me? I liked you. We could have been friends. But no, you had to close yourself off and be dishonest with me. I can't have dishonest friends, Sam. I need openness. I need intimacy."

Sam shook his head from side to side.

"You need a bullet in your head!"

Jerry went back to looking at the needle again. Then he picked up a bottle of alcohol and a clean dish rag.

"I'm going to forgive you for that, Sam. You know not what you do."

§ § §

As soon as Mark's face disappeared through the ceiling hatch, Natalie scooped up all the pieces to her cell phone to see if she could reassemble them and make a call. She quickly decided that it was hopeless. Then she moved over to the control panel and picked up the emergency phone. It rang and rang and rang but no one answered. She surmised that it must be patched into the main switchboard, which, after normal working hours would be routed into the guard desk. And Jamal was dead.

Natalie looked around the elevator. She tried to pry open the door with her fingers, but succeeded only in getting her shoulder to bleed again. Natalie plopped herself down on the floor again and then rummaged through her purse. And then a random thought occurred to her, *Mark placed the bloody knife back in its sheath on his belt without questioning how it had gotten there in the first place? How is that possible, unless a small part of him is aware of his actions?*

And then her thoughts went back to Sam Colton. What would he do in her situation? The thought flashed into her mind from no where. *First, he would pray.* She considered it a moment and then clasped her hands together. Normally she would close her eyes, but she was terrified and couldn't do it. She thought, *What if he comes back and I don't see him?*

"Dear God. Please help Sam Colton."

Natalie unclasped her hands and looked around as if surprised. *Where did that come from? Why was she praying for Sam?* She should be praying for Amethyst or for herself. She shook her head in confusion. It was as if her heart knew something that her head did not. So she clasped her hands and prayed again.

"Dear God. Please help Sam Colton. I don't care how you do it. Just send him help. Please save Sam Colton's life."

Natalie's prayer was interrupted by a noise above the ceiling. Immediately her heart rate skyrocketed. Someone was above her. He was coming back. But which one was it? Mark? Or Kayne?

§ § §

Jerry poured alcohol onto the rag and carefully cleansed the needle. Then he held it up to the light again and examined it like a surgeon checking his scalpel.

"You see, Sam, God used to kill people all the time. He

235

would regularly purge the earth of all unrighteousness. Take for example Sodom and Gomorrah, and all the cultures that God commanded the Jews to destroy. He said, kill them all, even the women and children, and their livestock."

He turned and faced Sam for a moment.

"That's a powerful statement about the nature of sin, Sam. Sin is so potent that it has to be cleansed or the host, the carrier if you will, has to be destroyed. So in a manner of speaking, I'm doing everyone a favor. Once I cleanse Amethyst, she will not have to be destroyed by God. I'm a servant of the most-high God. Can't you see that?"

Sam shook his head from side to side.

"Amethyst is just a little girl. She's not filled with sin. You're doing this for no reason at all. If you have to purge someone, then purge me! I've lived a long life and I've got lots of sin in me."

Jerry smiled.

"That's very noble, but the Bible says that all have sinned and come short of the glory of God. There are none righteous, no, not even one!"

Sam struggled with his bonds again. He thought he was making some headway, if he could just keep him talking long enough maybe he could break free.

"Yes, that's true, but God doesn't need you to purge evil. He's already taken care of it. He sent his son to die on the cross as atonement for all our sins. That's what the Bible says, *For God so loved the world that he gave his only son that whoever believes on him should not perish but have everlasting life.*"

Jerry's smile faded away and was replaced with a pensive frown.

"No, I don't think so. The Bible says that there shall be no remission of sins without the shedding of blood. I am going to shed blood as I expel the evil from her body. It's the only way. The Bible says there is only one way, and this is the way. God told me so himself."

"How did you get it so twisted?"

Jerry cocked his head to one side and softly smiled.

"God told me you would ask that. He told me to tell you this, *No man is twisted who is consecrated before the Lord. No man is twisted who follows the straight and narrow path and who heeds the voice of God.* But you can't understand that because the sin has separated you from God. Therefore, you can't hear his voice like I can. Once I purge the sin from your body, then you will hear his voice too, and then you'll understand, and you will walk in his ways and you will hear the shepherd's call. You will recognize his voice. I'm sorry, I'm just following God's commands. Now will you please be quiet so I can concentrate on my work?"

§ § §

Mark stuck his head down through the hole in the ceiling. The grin on his face was the biggest she'd ever seen.

"Hi Natalie! I'm back! Did you miss me?"

Natalie's heart sank. Then, as his feet came down through the hatch, she reached over and grabbed her pistol off the floor. She remembered Sam saying in one of her classes. "Always keep your gun loaded and ready to use, because an empty gun is nothing more than a very expensive club."

Even though it hurt to do so, she squeezed the grip tightly in her right hand. The pistol was stainless steel and she could jab it into his eyes if she had to. If she blinded him with the barrel, then she could crush his larynx and he would suffocate.

Mark's feet landed on the elevator floor with a loud thud, causing the thing to shake and vibrate. When he looked up at her, his face reminded her of Jack Nicholson in one of her favorite movies, *The Shining*. She made a mental note to herself. *If I survive this, I will never watch that movie again!*

"What's the matter, Nat? Cat got your tongue again?"

Instinctively, she brought the gun up in front of her chest and aimed it at the center of exposed mass. He shook his head from side to side.

"Now, Natalie, you are really disappointing me. I thought we'd already had that lesson. Do I need to teach you about the pecking order again? Do I need to cut you?"

Mark reached back and pulled the big knife out of its sheath. He held it up and watched the blade glisten in the light.

"Do you know why I prefer a knife, Natalie? It's because it's more personal. I like close up and personal. It just seems to me that nothing is more personal than death, and I like to feel the blade go in, then I can twist it and push harder if I want. And I like the way the blood pumps up and splashes on my face, the way it does when I do it perfect."

Natalie yelled in her most commanding voice.

"I want to talk to Mark!"

Mark threw his head back and laughed.

"I'm sorry, Mark's not here, but if you'll leave a message, he'll get back to you as quickly as is practical. Please speak plainly and articulately, and talk as long as you like."

Then he spoke as he leaned forward.

"Okay, that's long enough. BEEP!"

Natalie pulled the trigger.

BANG!

She felt the recoil in her hands and dropped the gun onto the elevator floor. What happened?

§ § §

Jerry turned away from Sam and blocked out his screams. He moved up to Amethyst's head and carefully turned it over to one side.

"God no! Don't let him do it! Don't do it!"

Jerry put the needle down while he pulled on a pair of latex gloves. Then he poured alcohol onto a gauze pad and meticulously swabbed the little girl's temple.

"Damn you! Stop it! Stop it right now!"

He picked up the needle again and felt the insertion point with one hand while bringing the point of the needle down with the other. As the needle touched her skin, Jerry whispered out loud, "There shall be no remission of sins without the shedding of blood."

Jerry didn't feel the 220-grain round nose bullet slam into the side of his head. Half his brain splattered onto the far wall, while the remainder of his head slumped down onto the desk and then followed his body to the floor.

Sam stopped screaming and his muscles relaxed for a moment. He looked around the room, but saw no one else.

"What the hell?"

§ § §

Natalie looked up at all the smoke rising around her. The sound had been deafening, and the first thing she'd thought was, *Where did that noise come from?* and her second, *Where did the smoke come from?*

Mark had fallen back onto his butt and now sat there two feet away with a confused look on his face.

"Where did you get the bullet?"

Natalie didn't say anything. She didn't know what to say. She was as confused as he was.

"Why do my legs feel numb? I can't move my legs!"

And then Natalie knew.

"It was a spine shot."

Mark cocked his head to one side again and rage filled his face.

"You bitch! You shot me in the guts and now I can't walk! I'm going to kill you!"

He tried to lunge forward but simply tottered off to one side like a drunken Kewpee doll. His head hit the floor with a thud. He fumbled with his hands to retrieve the knife, but Natalie simply moved to the far corner of the elevator where he couldn't reach her.

"Get back here! Get back here now!"

He thrashed on the floor for a while and then Natalie watched as Mark's eyes drifted shut and the knife slipped from his grasp and reluctantly fell to the floor.

§ § §

Roger Cornby sat high off the ground in the bucket of his John Deere front-end loader. It was an older model and it had been broken down for the past two months. Lucky for Sam Colton, Roger had just finished fixing the hydraulics the day before.

He had a perfect view of Sam's office window from here and he smiled to himself, speaking out loud to no one in particular.

"Now that was a damn fine shot if I do say so myself!"

He set his hunting rifle on his lap, being careful not to bump the scope. Then he ejected the empty brass and watched as it bounced around the inside of the steel bucket. He reached into the front pocket of his dirty bib overalls and pulled out a small bottle of muscatel. Slowly unscrewing the cap, Roger took a long drink and then replaced the cap and put the bottle back into his bibs. He let out a tired, very heavy sigh.

"Well, guess I'd better head on over there and bury the bastard."

Chapter Forty-Eight

Natalie sat back heavily against the elevator wall totally exhausted physically and emotionally. A tear ran down her cheek and off onto the bloody blouse, but it was all she could muster. She was alive and Mark could be dead for all she knew, but that came as little consolation to her. The last time she'd heard from Sam he was ... well, she didn't really know what had happened to Sam, but she knew it wasn't good. And as far as her mother and her little girl, all she could remember was what the strange voice on Sam's cell phone had told her.

"Sam is going to die. I'm pretty sure your mom is going to die too. And as for Amethyst, well, I just might have a more righteous need of her than you do. I might let her live, but we'll just have to see."

"Why God? Why does all this stuff happen to me?"

But there was no answer but silence. She wanted to scream and lash out at God for all the pain she'd suffered, but there was no more strength left in her. She'd lost a lot of blood.

"Natalie?"

Natalie looked up toward the ceiling, expecting to see God coming down to answer her, but there was nothing but bare elevator ceiling.

"Natalie?"

She looked over at Mark's body. He was still alive. Alive, but paralyzed and harmless.

"Yes, Mark, what do you want?"

He was lying on his back in a pool of his own blood with his head off to one side. His eyes were open and he was looking at her with those pleading, blue eyes of his.

"Natalie, do you think I'm going to hell now?"

Natalie slid herself slowly over to his side and looked down at him with newfound pity.

"I don't know, Mark. What do you think?"

He coughed and a little bit of blood foamed up and spilled down his cheek. Natalie took her left sleeve and wiped it off.

"Thanks. You really are a very good person, Natalie. That's why I like you so much."

The more he spoke, the more Mark's chest wheezed inside.

"Someone once told me that God doesn't send personalities to hell, only souls. And I was just wondering ... will you please pray for my soul?"

Natalie looked down on him and nodded.

"Sure. I'll do what I can. You should close your eyes though."

Mark's eyes closed and Natalie spoke without emotion. It was just an action that she didn't want to do, but that she knew she could live with later on, provided she lived at all.

"Dear God. Please help Mark's soul. I don't know what he needs, but I suspect that you do. So please do what needs doing. Thank you. Amen."

Mark's eyes opened and he looked up at Natalie and smiled.

"I just want you to know one thing, Natalie."

Natalie forced herself to reach down and brush the hair out of his eyes.

"And what's that, Mark?"

"My brother's keeper. I put one bullet back."

Mark's chest heaved up and then back down again several times. He coughed and Natalie held onto his shoulders. Somehow, his hand got into hers and she felt him squeeze hard. Then he grew quiet again for a moment. He opened his mouth and air came out, but Natalie couldn't make out what he was saying. She bent her ear closer to him.

"All ... by ... my ... "

Then, as she hovered over him, his hand relaxed and his eyes stared out into nothingness.

Natalie smiled ... and then she cried.

Chapter Forty-Nine

*"In the land of play,
in the land of dreams,
it's always fun or so it seems."*

Natalie sat on one of the larger headstones as Amethyst played off to the right of her, jumping from one stone to the next, singing all the while.

It had been a week since the elevator, and Natalie would have to go back to work soon. She hated the idea of it, going back to the place where she'd killed a man, where he had died in her arms. If everyone thought she was a freak before, what would they think now?

"I thought I would find you here."

Natalie jerked her head to the left and sent a sharp pain through her shoulder as Sam Colton walked up behind her.

"Oh, hi Sam."

Amethyst rushed over and jumped into his arms. He picked her up and swung her around twice and then threw her up in the air and caught her.

"Hello, my little princess. How are you today?"

"Doin' good. Just playin' in the park with mommy!"

"Well that's wonderful little one! How are your Barbie dolls today?"

Amethyst nodded her head up and down smiling all the while.

"They're good. Barbie's mad at Ken though cuz he stayed

out too late."

Sam laughed.

"Well, I'm sure the two of them will work it out."

He gave her a hug before setting her gently back down on the ground.

"Why don't you go on back to play while your mommy and I have a little chat."

Amethyst laughed as she ran away.

"Okay, but I want ice cream!"

Sam smiled after her and then his face turned serious as he sat down on the grave stone beside Natalie.

"You brought your daughter to the cemetery and she thinks it's a park?"

Natalie didn't answer him right away. She sighed heavily and then waited a few seconds more.

"I just got stabbed by a serial killer, and I don't feel like a lecture today, Sam. Can you skip to the short version?"

Sam reached up and rubbed his whiskered cheek with his right hand. He had a Band-aid on his hand and another on his temple.

"How's the stitches coming along? You healing up okay?"

Natalie looked off in the distance as she spoke. The tree leaves were fluttering as the breeze kicked up around them.

"Yeah. I'll be okay. Hurts a lot, but now it's itching, so I know it must be healing okay." Then she looked over at him. "What about you?"

"I'll be okay. Just a few bruises and cuts. Could've been worse. How's your mom handling it?"

Natalie smiled softly.

"My mom's a nut case. She was scared when it all happened, but now she can't stop blabbing to her friends about how she was kidnapped by the Vanilla Killer and held at knife point. I can't believe how she's acting. She was unconscious almost the whole time."

Sam ran his forefinger across one of the scratches on his hand.

"It's probably best that way. I'm glad Amethyst was out the whole time especially. She seems to be doing fine."

Natalie nodded and looked over at her little girl playing on the graves.

"Yeah, she's doing well. It was just a bad dream for her and she hardly remembers it. I think so long as I don't make a big deal about it, she'll be just fine. I just have to keep my mom's mouth shut about it, that's all. It'll be okay."

Sam was quiet for a moment.

"Hank Holden's grave is about hundred yards that way. He was a good man."

Natalie put her arm around Sam's shoulder and winced as she stretched the wound.

"I wish I could have known him. I really do appreciate that he was trying to protect me. I do, Sam, I really do."

Sam's eyes misted over but he quickly choked the feelings back down where they belonged.

"I blame myself. It was poor judgment on my part. He wasn't up to it."

Natalie leaned in closer to him.

"You sound like an old fool, Sam. They were both vicious killers and no one is ever up to that. It's their fault and theirs alone. And I suspect they're paying for their sins right now as we speak. But ... "

Natalie hesitated and Sam smiled softly.

"I know what you're thinking and you shouldn't even go

there, girl. No one knows why. No one knows how people like Mark turn into animals. The experts have theories, but not even they know for sure. Your job was to protect yourself and your little girl and that's what you did. You should let God worry about the eternal question of *why*."

Amethyst continued singing and Natalie allowed herself to be distracted by it for a moment.

> *"In the land of play,*
> *in the land of dreams,*
> *it's always fun or so it seems."*

"I know you're right, Sam. But there's just something inside me that has to know why. I have to ask the question and search for the answers."

Sam drew himself slowly to his feet with a groan.

"Getting old really sucks!" Then he turned to her. "Listen, Natalie, I need a favor from you."

A look of surprise came over her face as she stood up and came to near eye-level with him.

"You need a favor from me? I can't imagine what I have that you might need."

Sam crossed his arms over his chest and looked off through the cemetery as he spoke.

"Yeah, well, any man who tells you he doesn't need anything is a liar. But listen, because I'm only going to ask you this the one time."

Natalie had never seen him this nervous before and it intrigued her.

"Hank Holden didn't have any relatives and he left his private eye company to me in his will. I need help running it."

Natalie smiled before meeting his gaze.

"Sam, no offense, but I'm not the secretarial type. Especially now after all that's happened. I don't think I'll even be able to go back to my old job without beating the crap out of my boss. He's such a pompous ... "

"Natalie! I don't need a secretary! I need a partner!"

Natalie's eyes widened.

"A partner?"

Sam shrugged and then shoved his hands into the front pockets of his jeans.

"You heard me. I need a partner and you're the person I'm asking."

Natalie turned away and thought for a moment.

"But, Sam, I don't know anything about being a private investigator. I don't know the first thing about it."

"The hell you don't, girl. How many times have you stared death in the eye these past few months? You got the right stuff and then some. It just needs a little bit of polish that's all."

Natalie moved her right hand up to stroke her chin as she thought.

"I don't know."

"What? You have a better offer from someone else?"

"No, Sam, of course not. I just don't know if I can do it."

Sam nodded.

"That's a good attitude to have. But there's nothing to be learned that I can't teach you. And, I suspect that you might teach me a few things as well."

Natalie's face grew pensive and then she smiled.

"How much does it pay?"

Sam pulled his hands out of his pockets and crossed them on his chest again.

"You get half the profit. That's what a partnership is. But I expect you to do half the work."

Natalie hesitated one last time.

"Okay! Okay! And you can bring Amethyst in to the office with you so she doesn't have to be at day care all the time!"

Natalie laughed out loud and shoved her right hand out towards Sam.

"Okay then, put 'er there, partner!"

Sam smiled, uncrossed his arms and then shook his new partner's hand.

"Alright then. Shall we seal the deal with some ice cream?"

Natalie laughed and looked over at her daughter playing amongst the graves. It was time to get her out of here.

"Hey, Amethyst. Are you ready for ice cream?"

The little blonde-haired girl squealed with delight as she ran over to her mommy. And as she ran, she sang to herself.

"In the land of play,
in the land of dreams,
it's always fun or so it seems."

And the ice cream never tasted so good.

Skip Coryell now lives with his wife and children in Michigan. He works full time as a professional writer, and "*Stalking Natalie*" is his seventh published book. He is an avid hunter and sportsman who loves the outdoors. Skip is also a Marine Corps veteran, a graduate of Cornerstone University, and the Chief Pistol Instructor for Ted Nugent United Sportsmen of Michigan. Skip is the former Michigan State Director for Ted Nugent's organization. He has also served on the Board of Directors for Michigan Sportsmen against Hunger as well as Iowa Carry Inc. He is a Certified NRA Pistol Instructor and Range Safety Officer, teaching the Personal Protection in the Home Course for those wishing to obtain their Concealed Pistol Permits (www.mwtac.com). He also teaches Advanced Concealed Carry Classes for the more seasoned shooter. Skip is the President of White Feather Press and the co-owner of Midwest Tactical Training. Skip is the founder of the Second Amendment March (www.secondamendmentmarch.com).

For more details on Skip Coryell, or to contact him personally, go to his website at www.skipcoryell.com (email: skip@whitefeatherpress.com).

Dedicated to my wife, Sara, as always for her unwavering support in my writing. Without her this book could not have been written.

I would like to thank the following people for supporting me in writing this novel:

Dr. Hadley Kigar

Dr. Dianne Portfleet

Dr. Terrance Portfleet

Mary Mueller

Thank you for your help and your encouragement. You are all dear and talented friends.

Other Books by Skip Coryell

We Hold These Truths
Bond of Unseen Blood
Church and State
Blood in the Streets
Laughter and Tears
RKBA: Defending the Right to Keep and Bear Arms

Order your copies today at www.whitefeatherpress.com
or call 1-800-BookLog
or email at Orders@bookmasters.com
40 to 50% discounts for wholesalers, retailers and libraries.

Made in the USA
Charleston, SC
24 September 2016